TEST DRIVE

The Bachelor Series Book 1

Avonlea Cole

ONE

"HI! MY NAME IS . . ." No, that's not right. "Hello! I'm Drew, and I'm looking for love!" Ugh, I let out an exasperated breath and deleted the lines once again. When had it come to this? Putting an ad on a local site to try to find just one girl I could spend some time with; one I wouldn't despise after just a few weeks of dating. Well, before you pick up your pitchforks, let me explain. My story isn't all cupid and fairytales.

My real name is Wyatt Andrew Sloane II, but you can call me Drew. I could be called wealthy, not rock star wealthy, but I have my own plane. My parents happen to own a whole fleet of planes and the family business is doing . . . umm . . . well. Now most of you might think that being rich is easy; like I just float around on clouds all day drinking martinis, but the real story is that I spend most of my days ignoring phone calls and deleting emails from the many women out there hoping to land a wealthy benefactor.

My parents met before the money flowed in. My dad was a pilot, and my mom was a flight attendant so you can imagine how their love story played out. *I want that.* I want to find a woman that sweeps me off my feet like in the love stories, but the trouble is—I don't know what kind of girl I want.

It hit me a few weeks ago after a rough break up with my most recent girlfriend Camille. She cried, and well, I stood there like an idiot saying it wasn't her, it was me. I really meant that though. I am sure one day this super-hot model was going to take some guy by the balls and make him hers. Not me though. I want something else. It wasn't until I was recovering at a local bar with my friend, Matt, that I realized that I had it all wrong. The last five girls I had dated since high school were all socialites, that fashionista princess type that thought the best date was sitting by a runway picking out her "wedding dress" for our marriage that I hadn't even asked for. Whoa, right?

Matt had a great idea. "Hey dude, you should get on one of those sites—you know the dating ones? I wouldn't say who you are though. Just try some new girls, like test driving a new car?" His arm extended as he navigated the imaginary steering wheel through the crowd of patrons. Brilliant, right? Suddenly I had a plan. I planned to find different types of girls; maybe dating them briefly, but ultimately I wanted to find someone who meant something to me. Maybe I'd be into cowgirls, yeah, maybe the ones with the boots and the sexy hat. Or maybe I needed an ambitious woman who could fend for herself? I wanted to get started immediately, but I didn't think in my buzzed state of mind that my profile would be very attractive so I put the plan on hold for a day or two.

And now here I sit trying to type my name for God's sake. If I can't make it past this part then how in the hell am I going to put enough *non-loser* things in there to attract the right kind of girl, whoever she may be? I had to get my game together. I didn't want to feel so pressured, but with my parents pushing for me to settle down and my thirtieth birthday rolling in, my days as a rich playboy were numbered.

I put my hands on the keyboard and began to type. The lines flowed . . .

"Hey ladies! My name is Drew. I am a twenty-nine year old business man looking to settle down." Thankfully the list of questions provided gave me a guideline to go from. What types of personalities do I like in women? Hmmm, I had no response. I decided that was the best way not to limit the responses. "I am not sure what kind of woman I want, obviously, the basics like loyal and committed, but beyond that, I am open."

My Best Feature: "Ha! What's not to like?" I smirked to myself. "I am very outgoing." That seemed good enough.

My Favorite food: Duh! "Pizza—not just any pizza—New York style pizza with all the toppings." I hit the next button before I changed my mind. Honesty was so important with these questions, and well, what guy doesn't love pizza?

I answered what seemed like a bazillion others. I finished the forty-page questionnaire and went to upload a picture for my profile. I stopped short deciding against anything with an airplane or mansion in the background. I knew it would be necessary to rent another house since bringing them home to my wing of the million-dollar mansion was out of the question.

I uploaded a picture I had taken at a charity event not long ago. You couldn't tell where I was, but I was wearing a T-shirt, jeans, and boots. As soon as I hit the *complete profile* button, my screen froze. "You have got to be kidding me." I said out loud to a thankfully empty room.

The computer took a few minutes to load, and my patience was ready to give up on this dating site altogether. There must be other ways like speed dating or maybe the mall? Both ideas sounded horrible even as the thoughts crossed my mind.

Finally the screen came back to life, and I realized why it took so long—there were forty-seven pages of potential matches. Maybe I should have been more specific. I popped the top on a beer and sat back in my chair. This was going to take a while.

The site allowed you to *X* off anyone you didn't like and *Like* the ones you wanted to want to revisit. I won't lie, some of the people that came across the screen were not my type, and I could see that immediately, but there were quite a few that caught my eye. I made it through about twenty pages before my eyes started to cross and the girls started to look like blurs of bleach blonde hair. I decided to get up and stretch. I made a trip down to the kitchen and made a sandwich.

It was about nine thirty p.m. and usually I'd just be leaving the house to go meet some friends, but today I was on a mission. Who would have thought that searching for girls would be so hard? Forty-seven pages, really?

I returned to my computer with a fresh beer and a full stomach. I sat down and began to click. It took another hour to finish narrowing down the list, and by the end, I had six pages—over 30 women—of likes. Again I knew that was too many. I decided to narrow it down to ten, and who knew if they would even respond. I began clicking on the profiles. I took a few more off based on their questionnaire.

Amy, the dentist, put that she was a total neat freak and wanted a man who shared that trait. Nope—next. Candy, retail associate, totally loved blah blah and Gucci. Next.

Chelsea, the pediatrician, put that she loved kids and helping people in need, even did some volunteer work. Maybe. I clicked on her picture. She was a tall woman with black hair. She wasn't wearing a lot of makeup, and she was wearing her lab coat with a collared shirt. She looked smart. Nothing wrong with smart and caring. I quickly sent her a message to contact me and moved on.

I rolled through a few more that were *X'd,* and I started to feel like maybe I was being too picky. Next up was Jenna, the yoga instructor, says she loved anything to do with competition and extreme sports. She even used to be on the US ski team before an injury. Her long blonde hair hung to her waist in one picture where she was posing with some other instructors. A few others showed her rock climbing and sky diving. It was kind of hot! I sent her a message and continued my search.

It was kind of fun looking at all the answers the women had put. Some put my answers to shame. Next up was Violet. I almost hit the *X* button when I saw the cross and the word "virgin" pop up, but I held off. She looked sweet. And even though she wasn't my type in several ways, the whole point of this site was to meet someone new. I had begun copying and pasting the messages as it took too long to write individual ones.

Then there was Sarah, Tammy, Allison, and whatever the hell Kamya was. Another set of girls that were too far out there. I stopped on Victoria. In her picture she was holding one small, beautiful little girl. The thought of children scared the hell out of me, but she seemed nice in the picture, and eventually I wanted kids so I needed the "motherly" type. I sent her the copied message.

The next profile caught my eye for several reasons. The picture showed a girl looking down at the ground. Her face looked sad, like she was grieving someone or something. I couldn't say why I wanted to meet her. Maybe it was to take the pain away or see if somehow I could help? I messaged her and leaned back in the chair studying her face for a few minutes, taking a break from my hunt. Her name was Sicily, which I found rather odd, but different.

With only two pages left, I began to feel anxious. I wanted so badly to pick a variety, that way maybe I could discover which kind of girl made me happy. On this page only two names stood out, Amelia and Olivia. Amelia was an editor for a book publishing company in the next city over, and Olivia was a downright gorgeous girl who worked as a model. I knew I shouldn't pick her. I had dated a bunch just like her, but those piercing gray eyes were not easily forgotten, and I couldn't stop myself from sending the message.

I decided to contact all three girls on the very last page no matter what their profiles said. Christa, Georgia, and Claire were all messaged. This last set was a true variety from a country girl to a chef. I felt pleased at my choices. Now I had to wait. Patience wasn't exactly a virtue I had been blessed with. I skipped to my message box, which was of course empty.

My bed was calling my name, and as sleep crept in, I couldn't help but smile thinking of all the possibilities ahead of me.

TWO

I RAN TO MY COMPUTER the next day when I rolled out of bed around noon. I immediately logged in and checked my inbox. Nothing . . . Zero . . . Nada . . . I tried to calm my thoughts as I immediately started to regret my choice. Maybe they just hadn't checked their profiles. All the women had jobs! I decided to give it a day or two before I really freaked out. I hopped in the shower and got dressed for work, briefly stopping in front of the mirror as I admired my wardrobe. I could pull off the suit look for sure, but could I make a cowboy hat look natural? I was pretty sure cowboys didn't have their hair slicked back with gel.

Right then I knew that I would have to expand my personal appearance to make whoever I went out with comfortable, especially since I needed to appear average.

The drive to work was distracted, to say the least. Upon my arrival I couldn't have explained what the weather was like or the traffic flow. These women and the whole idea of opening up my future were consuming my everyday life. I tossed the keys to the valet and ascended the escalator two steps at a time. I bounded past the receptionist and immediately sat down at my computer to—dun dun dun—check my inbox. "Nothing." I pouted.

"Mr. Sloane, your father would like to see you." Beth, my father's secretary, had popped into my office without me noticing.

"Does he know I just came in?" I said with dread.

"Yes, sir. He said he wanted to meet with you as soon as you arrived."

"Well, please tell him I will be right there." I slid back from my desk and gave one last click to refresh the page. Nothing. I was becoming some sort of masochist forcing myself to stare at the empty screen.

I jetted down the long, narrow hall, decorated with old parts of planes and alternate flying vessels. My father was a collector of sorts, especially of fighter jet parts from the different wars. Much to his displeasure, I had no interest in flying planes. In fact, I was not a big fan of flying period. I much preferred long drives and road trips with stops along the way. I entered his office and sat in one of the plush leather chairs seated in front of his gray, steel desk.

"Father, you wanted to see me." My dad was staring intently at his computer screen, most likely studying weather patterns for the upcoming flights.

"Yes, son, I am glad you could join us before the day ended. Why must you be late when you know the other employees have a hard enough time doing their job and yours?" His gruff voice made me want to roll my eyes, but instead I gulped down my response.

"Well, father, I was up late last night working on a project, but I will try my best to be on time."

My father's eyes rose, lifting his sagging brows. "I take it that was not a work project, am I right?" I shrugged my shoulders and sucked in my cheeks. "Try, huh? Let's put it this way. You are here on time from now going forward *or* I will dock your pay a hundred dollars for each hour that you miss."

"I don't even make a hundred dollars per hour. That is preposterous!" I knew that whatever I said next made no difference. The old man was stubborn, and this company meant everything to him. Even more than his only child.

"Well then, I guess it is in your best interest to be on time." He went back to his computer. He sucked in his breath to speak, and I thought surely he would say something more sensible, but instead he boomed, "Beth! Get me Richard at the weather station on the phone. I need him to look over these reports for me."

I took that as my cue to leave. I was still fuming when I got back to my desk. I suppressed the urge to throw something at the all glass room. I knew he was right, but was it that big of a deal? It's not like he had given me any real responsibility. I was the supposed to be the head of marketing, but he insisted that he handle all the major clients personally. Until the old man was ready to hand over the reins, my job here was limited.

I straightened in my chair and flicked on the computer. My work email was virtually empty, and my desk sat barren of any work. *Great! So now I have to be here early to do nothing all day.* I let my mind wander to the beautiful ladies and their wildly different profiles. Their paths led in all different directions, and I wasn't sure which direction I wanted to head in first. Against what I knew was my better judgment, I clicked onto my profile again. There were over fifty views for my profile, but no messages. I read over my answers again, editing along the way. My answers were a bit short in comparison to the ladies' profiles.

"You've got mail!" my computer sounded off. A *one* popped up next to my message button. I hurriedly clicked on it in hopes of meeting my new lady.

"Welcome to findtheone.com, we have seven new listings for you!"

"Dammit!" I breathed out. I still had not gotten a message back from the women I emailed. I scrolled through the next seven ladies. I almost messaged them all, but there was only one I found remotely attractive. Her name was Caroline, and she was an attorney. She only had one picture which showed off her short brown bob style haircut and a set of very long legs. "I could use a good attorney in my life!" I snickered.

Beth returned just in time to see the cat-like grin on my face. "Well I can see that you have nothing but time on your hands. Your father asked me to drop these off to you. It's a list of potential clients, and he wants you to look them over and make the initial contact to set up business meetings with your father." She laid the thick files on my desk and exited in under twenty seconds.

It sounded like a job for the secretary. I knew my father didn't trust me enough to handle anything important on my own, and I wasn't begging for extra work by any means, but this just seemed like busy work. I finished typing a quick message to Caroline and tackled the list of names.

"Uh yes, this is Wyatt Sloane with Sloane Aeronautics, and I was hoping to reach Mr. Bingham." I tapped my pencil on my desk while the receptionist put me on hold. I had my father's calendar pulled up along with the idiot proof tags where he wanted the meetings to be held.

"Mr. Bingham, this is Wyatt Sloane with Sloane Aeronautics. My father would like to know if you would be interested in meeting him one day this week to discuss flight options for your company." I waited and listened as the old man hummed his way through his calendar. I scheduled the meeting for lunchtime on Thursday at the Maribel Country Club. When we hung up, I repeated the call to different executives, and when I was finished—a whole fifteen minutes later—I turned my attention back to my inbox.

To my surprise there was a response. I was even more surprised when I saw that it was from Sicily. I remembered her as the fragile broken girl in the picture, and her response left me questioning what she might be like away from the computer.

"Hi Drew! I got your message, and I wanted to maybe chat sometime. I don't usually like going out with people I haven't spent some time getting to know. I read through your profile and saw that we have quite a bit in common. Can I ask you why you picked me to respond to? Anyway, I hope to hear back from you, if you are still interested.
-Sicily"

I immediately wanted to respond, but would it make me look desperate? Did I even have an answer to her questions? I wasn't used to a woman who lacked so much confidence in themselves, and I had to admit I already felt pressured to be some savior that could fix probably years of decay. I took a chance though. Maybe being the support for someone was the change I needed?

"Sicily, I am very glad that you wrote me back. I would love to chat with you when you are available. I picked you because of your picture actually. You have that Mona Lisa stare, and I couldn't look away. I am interested in meeting with you. You can reach me at 828–555–4213 if you want to talk.

-Drew"

I hit the send button and turned my chair around to face the window. The sun was beginning to set behind the mountains, and the other staff started to leave. I packed up my stuff and headed back down the long hallway to my father's office.

"Sir? Do you have a minute?"

He nodded and motioned for me to come in but did not look away from his computer. "I finished setting up the meetings for you."

"Good. Thank you." His gruff voice showed his distraction. "Is there something else?" His ice cold blue eyes darted over to me.

"I wondered if you would allow me to sit in on the meetings with you. Maybe then I could get a feel for what needs to happen."

"You would be interested in that?" He lifted his eyebrows in surprise.

"Yes, father. I have noticed that my duties here are more like busy work, and I would prefer to take on a more important role if I need to be here every day."

"Well yeah, son, you can add the meetings to your calendar, and I *expect* you to be there." He turned his attention back to the computer, and I showed myself out.

I couldn't remember my dad ever being this disconnected when I was a child. Of course his company had not exploded into what it is now until I was a teenager, and I spent most of my time away for college. I knew that

I had disappointed him when my path didn't lead directly to the pilot industry, but to be honest, heights scared the hell out of me. My dad couldn't understand that I much preferred business and marketing to weather patterns and flight schedules. Not that he would ever let me handle that stuff anyway. My mother understood, at least. She had begged my father to retire and travel the world with her, but he couldn't let it go.

I had just sat down in the driver's seat of my old, but fully restored, Nova when the phone rang. I checked the number, but it came up blocked. Normally that call would go to voicemail, but since it could be Sicily I answered.

"Hi, this is Drew!" I tried to sound perky, but it came out as a yell over the roaring engine.

"Hello, this is Sicily. Umm, you gave me your number so I thought I would call, but if you are busy, just forget it." I could barely understand her whispered words so I cut the engine off and apologized.

"I'm sorry, my car is loud, and the echo in the parking garage would about deafen you. You said this is Sicily, right? I'm glad you called." She was quiet for a moment like she was immediately regretting making this phone call. "Sicily, are you still there?"

"Yes, I'm here. What kind of car do you have?" She sounded as unsure as her picture looked, and I did my best to make her feel comfortable.

I told her about my car and bits about the company I worked for, making sure to leave out the name. For over an hour, I sat in the garage talking with her about our likes and dislikes. She told me that she was a librarian, which was different than anyone I had ever dated. She was obviously into books and poetry. I couldn't say I shared that interest, but I kept reminding myself that I wanted different.

"Have you met a lot of people on this site? I am new to this, and I am not really sure how this works." I was being totally honest when I said that.

"Umm sort of. I mean I have messaged with guys, but I haven't made it to the date part. Either they lose interest or I find them creepy, but I read that you should know how you feel about someone in three dates."

"Oh really?" I laughed. "I am intrigued, please explain what you mean."

"Yes, I read once that you should meet first in public for dinner or coffee or something, and then the second the girl should pick the date, and the third the man should choose the date. Both should pick based on what kinds of things they enjoy, and by the end of the third date you should know where you stand." Her voice sounded like she read the words straight out of a fairytale.

"I like that! Actually that is brilliant." And I just found my new motto. Who couldn't survive three dates?

I could hear the smile in her voice when she said, "Really?"

"Yes, ma'am." I could hear a giggle escape from her mouth. "So how about it then? Wanna have date one?"

"Um sure, when?" she said. She sounded so shy and quiet. I wanted to see that smile in person.

"How about tonight?" I took a few breaths, and I could hear her withdraw from the phone. "Just for dinner. I give you my word that I am not a stalker, crazy person, or weirdo. Scout's honor!"

"Were you a boy scout?" she said.

"Well no. But I do stand behind my word. How about this? You pick the place and time. I will get there early, and you can check me out. If you don't like what you see, you can leave, and I will understand."

"All right, I guess. Um, eight thirty at Nina's Pizza on Main Street?" Her voice still didn't sound certain, but I guess it could be risky meeting a stranger for the first time.

"I have never been there before. That's perfect, I will be there. Talk to you soon." We said our goodbyes, and I fired up the engine. According to my navigation system the restaurant was almost an hour away, and I still had to get home to change.

THREE

I ENTERED THE RESTAURANT and scanned the crowded room for her face. I was early as promised, but the front entryway was swarming with people. I pushed through and waited at the front desk for someone to lead me to a table. I felt overdressed in my khaki pants and Italian Cashmere sweater. I hadn't realized that the restaurant might not be four stars, but the food smelled amazing. I could practically taste the oozing cheese and the lightly roasted toppings from halfway across the room.

I stood there like an idiot waiting for someone to seat me until a waitress pointed to the sign that read: "Please seat yourself." I was glad at that moment that I had arrived early before she could see me struggle to find a booth on my own. A waitress finally rescued me and showed me to a table in the back of the restaurant. I told her I was waiting for someone, and she disappeared into the crowd.

I looked around studying all the decorations that lined the wall. Several pizza relics, some football jerseys, and a huge poster showing all the toppings you could ever think of putting on a pizza. I checked out the menu to see what my options were, smirking as I noticed all the pizzas were named after cities in America and several countries around the world. There was a sign at the bottom boasting the no silverware rule. I looked around to see how that was working out for the customers trying to slide the mounds of toppings in their mouths with no silverware to catch it. The customers at the surrounding tables all had napkins stuffed down their shirts, and they were rolling and folding their pizzas to keep it all in.

I glanced up at the entrance just in time to see a petite brunette squeeze through the crowd. She was wearing a knee-length purple floral dress with a long-sleeved gray sweater. She wore black flats exposing her lily white legs. I couldn't tell through the dark rimmed glasses if the shy beauty was in fact Sicily, but when her face turned red as she scanned the room I knew it must be her. She was pretty, not gorgeous, but definitely cute. I waved her over, and she looked down at her feet like she was trying to convince herself to go through with the date.

I stood as she approached our table. "Sicily, right? I'm Drew. It's nice to meet you."

I reached to shake her hand, and she extended her hand slowly. I had thought about kissing her hand, like a gentleman of course, but decided against it. She looked petrified, in total disbelief over the fact she was here. I couldn't pinpoint whether that was a good or a bad sign.

"So have you been here before?" I asked trying to break the awkward silence.

"Yes, many times. They have great pizza." She made eye contact when she spoke but then went right back to the menu hiding her light brown eyes.

"Wonderful! What do you usually get?" I clasped my hands together on top of the menu giving her my full attention.

"Well, normally I get the Kitchen Sink Pizza." I was shocked. I looked down at the menu and read off literally every ingredient they had.

"Wow, that must be a huge pizza. And you eat that yourself?"

"You can buy it by the slice, and I can normally eat two." She was smiling now at least. I hoped that she would break out of her shell a bit. I was not used to having to lead the conversation. Usually I was the one with the short answers.

The menu offered a variety sampler, The Tour of America, and it came with eight different slices. I couldn't deny that my appetite had built up thinking about the gobs of cheese I was about to inhale. Our food was delivered, and I continued to force the conversation. She was responding, but I could tell she was either very nervous or very uninterested. This strain made it difficult for me to get to know her, or maybe this was her. I couldn't imagine this being an everyday struggle, but she was sweet and smart, and I wanted to find out if she could be bold too.

She pushed her square black glasses farther up her nose and bit into her folded Philly style pizza. I watched the thick mozzarella cheese stretch down her chin. She quickly scooped up the cheese and twisted it into her mouth. Her thin lips curved into a quiet smile. I knew my staring was making her uncomfortable, but watching her cheeks flush and her eyes dart away was kind of sexy.

"Well, this place is awesome. I will definitely be back, although it's gonna take me a year to try all of the different pizzas." I laughed, stretching my arm across the booth. "We should do this again sometime."

"Yeah, I will call you. It's going to be a busy week at the library, but I'll be in touch." She quickly reached for her purse as the waitress dropped off the ticket.

"No, please." I stuck out my hand snatching away the receipt. "Allow me."

She only nodded in response and quickly stood from her seat. "I hate to rush off, but it's been a long day. It was a pleasure meeting you, Drew. Safe travels."

I swallowed the urge to call bullshit as she spoke.

It was around nine forty-five, and the party boy in me wanted to point out that the night wasn't even close to over, but she had to work the next day, and so did I. I briefly remembered my dad's warning. She thanked me and repeated her statement that she'd be in touch. She didn't wait for me to follow her out, and I didn't want to push into her comfort zone.

I was certain I'd blown it. I dropped a hundred dollar bill on the table and told the stunned waitress to keep the change. She quickly wrapped her arms around me; her swishing ponytail splashing the strawberry scented shampoo in my face. Briefly. *Briefly*, I thought about whether I could take her home instead. I could use a pick me up.

I no longer recognized the guy I was becoming. The old me wouldn't have blinked about possibly taking a hot waitress out for drinks or something a little hotter. The drive home was full of uncertainty. I wondered if maybe I was not her type or maybe I am not anyone's type. I was almost positive my last string of girlfriends were only interested in my money, and now with the girls not knowing, what if they weren't interested at all? It was a sobering feeling; one that I wasn't willing to linger on.

I pulled into the garage and parked the car giving the engine one last rev before shutting it off. I laid my head on the steering wheel feeling both exhausted and disappointed. The date with Sicily had gone okay, but I had no idea what she was thinking.

I wanted to be on time to work so I headed straight to bed. I didn't immediately fall asleep, and instead I decided to check my email one last time for any other responses. None!

Great, I thought, perfect ending to a rough day. I cranked up the wave machine next to my bed and drifted to sleep picturing myself in a better place.

The alarm came too early the next morning, but I forced myself to get up. By the time I walked through the doors at work, I felt totally refreshed. The other employees stared in disbelief when I rushed right to my mailbox in search of work to do. I came in today hoping to prove myself and well, to take my mind off my failing love life. I was starting to wonder whether I was cut out for this type of relationship or if I should stick with the mindless gold diggers? They did cater to my every whim—as long I paid for theirs.

No. I didn't want that anymore.

I sat down at my computer, and against my better judgment, I checked the inbox. This time there were two messages. My sullen mood picked up only to crash and burn. The first email was a response from Amelia, the book editor, and she replied with "Thank you for your inquiry, Drew, but I have recently moved to New York and just haven't updated my profile. Good luck!"

Wow, I thought, *my batting average was tumbling and if things didn't pick up who knows how desperate I'd get?* Email two was a response from Jenna, the yoga chick. I read her three sentence long reply. "Hey Drew! I'd love to get to know you better. Want to meet sometime?"

"I'd like to take you skiing, and I'd definitely like to see you . . ." I said aloud.

"Oh really, son, I didn't think you could handle the heights?" My father's voice boomed into my office causing me to almost choke on the words coming out next.

"Uh, father!" I desperately clicked out of the message and mindlessly stacked some papers on my desk. "What can I do for you?"

"Well, I can see you are here this morning . . . although who knows what you are working on? No matter. I wanted to know if you would be interested in coming to the board meeting this morning? We will be discussing employee benefits and some complaints from the staff."

"Sure! I'd love to. Where is the meeting being held?"

"It'll be in the conference room next to my office, and it starts at ten sharp." His no nonsense personality had always put me on edge. He had gotten rigid in his old age; well, I guess it started when the company took off. I no longer knew the man who came to all my baseball games and award ceremonies. He had even missed my college graduation because of a last minute flight issue with an important client.

I checked the clock; it was nine fifty. I quickly pulled the message up and sent a quick note back to Jenna. I listed my personal cell number and said she could call or text about where or when to meet. I grabbed a notepad and headed down the hall. I had never sat in on the meetings, so I had no idea how awesomely . . . *boring* it would turn out to be.

Two hours of my life that I would never get back. My stomach rumbled, and my fingers itched to slip the phone out of my pocket to look at anything, even just the deserted island screensaver. "Son, what do you think of the employee complaints? Do you think that we should accommodate their requests?"

Busted! What do I say? How could I answer a question I hadn't really heard? "I think that without the employees, this place could not run effectively so if there is something we could do to make their time here easier, then I say yes."

The bullshit I had just spewed out of my mouth seemed to have surprised the old man. "It sounds like you should handle the task. I want to appoint you to handle the rest of the employee evaluations, and you can manage their requests and see the process through. All right, gentleman, have a good lunch!"

Whoa, whoa! What had I just signed up for? I regretted zoning out the entire meeting. I should have given them a strict "No" and continued about my day. Bob, the employee benefits director, reluctantly dropped off the heaping pile of employee evaluations. He gave me a sad nod as he exited. I could tell he had no confidence in my ability to see this through.

I just read the top evaluation, which listed that there should be a machine with feminine products in each of the women's bathrooms. *Great. This was bound to be excruciating.*

I headed back to my office with the pile of complaints and slapped them down on the desk. Well at least I'd have something to keep me busy. I thought about Sicily's sweet smile from the night before. I tried to keep her polite personality in mind as I began reading through the outrageous complaints. They got worse. Everything from office supplies to a massage machine to put on the back of the chairs? I was beginning to feel like the employees were making this shit up just to be rude. I had been given control over this project, and I intended to weed out the ones that were too *out there.*

Jenna had asked me to join her for lunch at a local farmers' market. My morning had been spent doing—I kid you not—interviews with employees to figure out some kind of solution to their needs. Just shoot me now if I have to hear one more woman complain about her "sudden, without warning, heavy flow." Don't get me wrong, I wouldn't want to take their place for a minute. I had just not expected so much graphic detail poured into my brain like cement, giving me a *full* picture of the emergency. Another surprising detail was that apparently all the women felt the same way, which left me no other solution than to check on the cost of such an addition to our ladies' room.

My escape to lunch was well deserved. I only wished I could drum up some sort of appetite. I entered the farmers' market just in time to see Jenna ordering a salad from the deli. Her long hair was in a ponytail today and even then, it stretched way down her back. I stopped inside the door to admire the view before making my way to join her. I could only see her profile, but her dark blue yoga pants and white tank top showed everything I wanted to see. Her toned body and supple assets were mouthwatering and even from the side her smile was inviting. I strode up to the counter and introduced myself.

"Jenna? Hi, I am Drew; it's nice to meet you." I extended my hand, and she gripped it, rather tightly I might add.

"Oh wow, thanks for meeting me today. Sorry about my wardrobe, I was teaching a class at the gym, and I didn't have a chance to change. Please join me." She motioned to a table in the corner, and I said I'd be there shortly. I barely managed to breathe when she walked away. The tight pants formed to her every curve. *Women shouldn't do that to men*, I thought.

She took her seat at the small café table, and I snapped out of my trance. I ordered a chocolate-banana smoothie and made my way to our table. "This place is delish, right?" she said, dumping the container of granola onto her strawberry pecan salad. She didn't use any salad dressing, which struck me as odd, and instead squeezed a half of lemon over the kale leaves.

"Yeah." I motioned to my smoothie. "I don't think I've ever been here before actually." I tried to drink the too thick smoothie, but the little tid-bits making it through tasted of vitamins so I gave up pretty quickly.

"Oh really! Are you from around here?" She genuinely looked interest-ed which gave me hope considering the last *odd* date I'd had.

"I have lived in Raleigh most of my life actually. What about you?" I had stopped short of mentioning my dad's company and the necessity of living close to airports.

"Well, I am originally from Colorado, but I moved here a few years ago to attend college, and I fell in love with it." The way her eyes sparkled when she said how much she *loved* this state made me wonder how deeply she could *love* someone. "I still miss the mountains, but I don't miss the crazy weather patterns. It gets cold here but not that cold." She stirred around her plate before looking back up, directly into my eyes. "So what should I know about you?" I felt like she was peering into my soul, and I answered her question by spouting out my basic info minus how much money was in my bank account.

"I'm pretty normal." Depending on your version of normal. "I'm twen-ty-nine, and I work in business/marketing/personnel services. I like to go out to dinner and the occasional after party. I like to travel . . . by car most-ly, and I love the ocean."

"Interesting," she said, smiling and nodding her head.

I knew I had to turn on the charm so I flashed my best *interesting* smile and said, "Wait. What do you mean interesting? Interesting like cool or interesting like I am a weirdo?" We both laughed, and she took a sip of her drink.

"Well, I hate to break it to you, but interesting like I can't believe you didn't mention one outrageous thing in there. Are you hiding some bad boy lifestyle, or are you really a business man that likes to party on occa-sion?"

"I'm stunned!" I laughed. "If you're asking if I like jumping off build-ings or something I must warn you, I'm afraid of heights and I am not a fan of most things life threatening, but I am willing to go for a thrill ride every now and then."

"Fair enough," she said. We discussed her background in depth. She had graduated from U.N.C. here in North Carolina with a degree in sports medicine and education. Now she was an instructor for an extreme sports company in Raleigh that does everything from rock climbing to hot yoga. My mind roamed thinking of whatever "hot yoga" consisted of. I was impressed, a little thrown, but very impressed.

"So where do we go from here, Drew? I have to get going, but I'd like to see you again." Her piercing green eyes weren't riddled with shyness or fear, instead she looked like a girl who knew what she wanted, and that confidence was very appealing. So I explained my newly adopted three-date rule.

"Okay then. So the next date is my choice. You're sure you aren't scared of what I might pick?"

"Actually I am a bit scared, but I want to find someone that can keep me interested and someone I am compatible with so I am willing to try new things . . . except for the heights. No sky diving if you can resist." She giggled and said she'd try. I don't know if I believed her, but we would cross that bridge when we got there. I tossed our mess in the trash and walked her to her car. Well, I thought it would be a car, but then again I should have known. On this beautiful summer day, Jenna had driven her motorcycle to work. According to the black decals on the blinding white painted motorcycle it was a Yamaha R1. Her helmet was also white with a swirly black design and her matching leather jacket completed the look. Freaking hot!

I watched her mount the crotch rocket, and my mind roamed to the dark side thinking about how those long legs would feel mounted around me. When the motor roared to life, I had to adjust my pants. She looked back at me one more time; I could still see her glowing green eyes through the tinted helmet. I waved and she sped off around the corner.

Damn, that girl was fine.

I was getting warmer. The library chick might have failed, but this girl was a prize.

When I finally made it back to the office I was a few minutes late, but I had worked constantly through the morning so I hoped it wouldn't matter.

I went back to work reading through the files coming to the quick conclusion that I needed some sort of estimate. I pulled up one of our vendor sites and looked up the dreaded feminine product machine. Turns out it wasn't that expensive. It was more for the refills than the machine, but if we needed to we could refill them ourselves and skip the maintenance fee. I wonder who would be in charge of that task.

I got the quotes together and considered that issue dealt with until the next board meeting convened in two weeks. Moving on to another office request, I totally agreed that the snack machine situation was monumental. The request was made for new snack vendors to be brought in. The snack machines were ancient, and I had refused to buy anything from them because the last bag of M&Ms I'd purchased were not only out of date, but they had turned completely white in color. *Gross.* I contacted a local vendor, and he said he would come down with some options tomorrow at ten a.m. I jotted it down on my calendar and moved on.

The rest of the day went like that. A few of the evaluations were funny. Jake, one of the pilots, had put that he would like a box of Swiss roll cakes available for every flight and new tassels for their uniforms.

I actually felt important doing this project, in fact, for the first time I felt like I had a sense of responsibility. I enjoyed fixing problems and finding ways to make our company a better place to work. I couldn't say I cared a lot about the flying part, but the employees were an important part of the company. *Maybe I could be their supervisor?* I would definitely bring it up to my father at the next board meeting. I mean we did have an employee relations manager, but he focused more on the insurance benefits and payroll. I put the thoughts aside and grabbed my things to leave. Then it hit me! I hadn't checked my inbox since the message from Jenna, almost eight hours ago. I could no longer wait till I arrived home. I clicked the link and watched it load. Three new messages appeared. The first was from Claire, she was the chef of a local hotel restaurant. I had been to a few catering events there, and the food was phenomenal.

"Hi Drew. Sorry for the delayed response, the hotel I work for has been booked solid for a few weeks, I would love to hear back from you and maybe schedule a time to meet for drinks or something. Anyway, talk to you soon." Her message was very pleasant, and I instantly responded with a no problem, blah blah blah, I'd love to meet her. I meant the words just the repeating them part was getting a little weird.

The second message was from Jenna, we had never exchanged numbers, and she was asking for mine. She said lunch was great, and she would be in touch about that second date. I messaged her back with my number and blah blah blah.

The last message was from Victoria. She was a single mom, and I had been nervous about being around her child. She wrote, "Drew, what a handsome name. I am sorry I took so long to respond. Life is busy when school is out. Maybe you could tell me a little bit about yourself? I am a single mom to a six year old. I work part time for the school system, and I also do side work during the tax season. Gotta make ends meet, right? I love reading and going to the movies and anything outdoors. I look forward to hearing from you! -Victoria"

The message was sweet, and I felt like I could picture who she was as a person. I wanted to meet her for sure. I messaged her back and once again shut my computer down.

FOUR

THE NEXT EVENING I headed out of the house to meet Matt. He was hanging at one of our favorite pubs, Sir Anthony's, watching reruns of UFC fights.

"Happy hump day, man," he said, standing to greet me. He smelled of hops and pretzel salt, and I could tell by the way he hugged me that he was well on his way to being toasted.

"All right, hero. Have a seat before you get knocked out early." I shrugged him off, and we sat down at the tall pub tables. Wendy, our favorite blonde waitress, came over with a tall glass of Samuel Adams. "Just the lady I was looking for." I smiled.

"Well, I know what my fellas like." She winked and twisted her hips walking away. I had a brief thing with her for a while, but we both decided that it couldn't go anywhere, especially since her boyfriend—I think his name was Jerk Off—tried to fight me outside the pub. *Yikes!* I smiled remembering the look on her face when she said "Friends?" Who could resist a hot blonde winking as she ended our umm, *friendship*.

"So where have you been all week? I haven't seen you once since last week," Matt slurred as he chugged the last swig or his foamy beer.

"At work, man. My dad came down on me about being late all the time. But I have to say that since I started getting into it, I kind of like the management side."

"Has he gotten over his dream of you flying yet? Lord knows he hasn't been the same. I saw him pass by the other day in one of those tinted black rides. He didn't even glance my way. He used to be like a dad to me growing up."

"Yeah, me too. Old man's gotta relax . . ." I jammed a pretzel rod into the honey mustard dip in the basket and chewed on the end. I let the salty goodness sink in putting some space in between the negative comment and the good news I had come to share. "So check this out." I whipped out my phone, and Matt leaned towards me. Pulling up my profile on the dating site, I scrolled through my profile showing him the pictures I'd chosen.

"Uh why are we looking at pictures of you?" he yelled far too loud as he grabbed for my phone. "I want to see some hotties, man."

"Patience!" I laughed pushing him away. "Okay. Check her out." I showed him the picture of Jenna knowing that he would be insanely jealous of my hot find.

"Dudeeee! I hate you so much right now. Leave it to you to find a babe on a dating site." Pouting, he jammed another pretzel rod in his mouth; the crumbs taking up residence in his bushy goatee. "But you got to watch out for the *catfish*."

"Catfish?" I exclaimed. "What the hell is a catfish?"

"You know. The people who put up fake pictures and when you meet them in person you're like '*WTF, you're a cow.*'" We both nervously laughed while I considered the risk I was taking with each date.

Shaking off the warning I said, "Well, this girl is no catfish. She drives a motorcycle, and she is an instructor for "hot yoga" among other things. She is smoking hot."

By the time we headed home, Matt could no longer walk. I dropped him off in front of his townhouse and waited until he stumbled inside. I got home just in time to catch Claire online. We messaged back and forth about our likes and dislikes. She was twenty-six and had graduated from culinary school. Food was her life apparently, and she was looking forward to expanding her social calendar. We decided to have dinner on Friday night, and I fell asleep smiling about Jenna and the other girls I was meeting. *Oooh, the possibilities.*

As promised, I attended the business lunch I had set up for my father with Mr. Bingham at the country club. The sun beating down on the all slate patio was nearly unbearable, but as I watched my father and the old man discussing trips they had taken and some of the war memorabilia that my father had managed to collect, I realized that so much of this business was dependent on the personal relationships he managed to maintain. Like a light bulb I continued to process the relationships in my personal life that I had maintained; next to none. There was my dad and that was about as solid as a piece of paper. My mother was probably my only true supporter in a lifetime full of so-called friends. Matt and a few other guys were good friends, but I needed someone lifelong that could have my back in times of need. Amazingly, I began to add items to my checklist of the type of girl that I wanted. No longer were looks and status as important as support and comfort. *I think I just became an adult.* I snickered to myself.

"Drew, I have a son about your age." He nudged my father's arm as he spoke, continuing on to say, "I wish I could get him out of bed before noon to attend a boring business meeting with us old timers." My father gave an uncomfortable laugh while rolling his eyes in the opposite direction. "Your father is lucky to have you, son."

The raspy cough my father barked out could be heard from the other side of the golf course. My blood boiled, just a bit, at the thought of him denouncing me in front of this potential client. "Well," I began to recover as this client had just paid me a compliment. "It's a tough world out there, and you have to stay current to stay in the game. I bet you and your son would thoroughly enjoy the new jet my father has designed. I haven't been able to see it firsthand, but the plans are amazing. It has every comfort that a man like yourself would need on that trip to Japan you are taking next month."

My father's bushy brows creased together as I spoke and then relaxed into a surprised awe as Mr. Bingham replied, "Right you are, son. I believe that I will take you up on that offer if the plane will be done in time."

"Wonderful." I stood next to the table and readied myself to leave. "Mr. Bingham, it was a pleasure meeting with you, and I hope that we will be together for years to come." We shook hands, and he grasped mine heartily. My lips dropped into a thin line as I made my exit. "Father." I only said the one word as I pushed through the patio gate leaving the outdoor eatery. He didn't bother to respond.

Embarrassing. That was the word I was looking for the full forty-five minute drive back to the office. What was the point of me attending the meetings if he constantly felt the need to express his utter disappointment in me? Why not just fire me and get it over with? I paced my office for a few moments, cursing as needed to deal with my anger.

Knock! Knock! Knock! The quick knock drew me out of my trance and before I could swallow my irritation I barked, "What?" I instantly felt remorseful for screaming at the unknown knocker, unless of course it was my father, in that case, he could just keep walking.

It wasn't my father. I should've known he wouldn't feel bad about his rudeness. Instead his secretary Beth peeked around my door. Her posture showing her concern at the tone I had just used. "It went that well, huh?" Usually she attended the meetings with my father and today when I had gone along, she did seem a bit . . . nervous. I assumed it was her lack of confidence in me which in all honesty may still be the case.

"Yeah. The meeting itself went great if you discount the total disrespect when it comes to his treatment of me. Maybe if I quit and become a client we can have a good relationship again." Wringing my hands together and the pace at which I was stalking across the room showed my anger, which on a normal day I would prefer to do in private. "I'm sorry, Beth. He just gets under my skin." I forced myself to sit in my chair and quickly scrubbed my hands over my face.

"Hey, you don't have to apologize to me. I know things are strained between you guys, but it'll get better. Just hang in there." The lopsided innocent smile she shot me was reassuring. Hell, she knew him better than I did. I was determined to end this streak of letting people down, including myself. I was—*am*—better than that.

When I opened my eyes, she'd already disappeared out of the office before I had a chance to thank her. I massaged the sides of my throbbing temples and turned my chair around to stare out of the window. A plane was boarding a few runways over. I watched as they shoved bag after bag into the storage area. So many suitcases for two people I had to wonder how long they intended to be gone. When the plane's doors shut and the plane began to move, I had to look away. The takeoff was always my worst fear. The odds of a crash were so much more likely to happen on takeoff or landing.

I heard the door click open, and I turned just in time to see Beth returning with a cup of coffee. "You like it black, right?" She sat the mug down on my desk and curiosity got the best of me.

"Yeah, how did you know?"

"Well, that's how your father likes it. You are more alike than you think, ya know?"

"I doubt that," I muttered. "But thanks for the coffee and the pep talk."

She nodded and then disappeared again. *Sweet girl. No wonder why my father likes her.*

I left before my father returned that evening, and I fully expected to pass him somewhere in the house. My mother had made chicken potpie for dinner, and I scooped out a large slice before retreating to my room for the evening. Beer and chicken potpie. *What a meal!*

Checking my messages, I had several texts from Jenna telling me "to get ready" and that she was "so excited to see me again." *Me too!* Conversations with Claire and Victoria had continued. Victoria seemed very down to earth and dedicated. I could use that. While Claire had a great work ethic and the way to a man's heart is through his stomach, right?

A few new girls had messaged me, but I quickly ignored them as the words *princess* and *diva* were mentioned in their profile a few *hundred* times. *No, thanks.*

"Andrew, can I come in?" The quiet voice was easily recognized as my mother.

"Sure," I said, less than enthusiastic about the Band-Aid she was getting ready to put on my father-son relationship issues.

"Son, look at this room. It looks like a dorm room in here."

"Well, I have been busy lately. I haven't had time to do my laundry in a while."

"Yes, I see and by a while you mean like months, right?" She smirked as I turned my attention from my computer screen to her gleaming blue eyes.

"Why don't we skip the pleasantries and you tell me why you are really here?" I raised my eyebrows looking past the sly smile on her face.

"Whatever do you mean, Andrew? Are you referring to the way you embarrassed your father at the meeting today?" She crossed her arms with concern written on her face.

"Is that what he told you? That lying . . ." Shaking my head fiercely as the list of names rolled through my head.

Her finger pointed directly at me as she warned, "Watch it, mister. I am just here to get to the bottom of all this hostility between you two. You two are family and you have got to get past all of this, especially if you are going to work together."

"I put forth the initiative to start attending the meetings as a show of faith that I was serious about the company. I have taken on several new projects, and I would like to think that I was very helpful in the meetings. Unlike him. He had the nerve to snicker when the client paid me a compliment. So if anyone was embarrassing it was *him.*" Huffing, I went back to my computer screen and tried to focus on anything but the disapproving frown on my mother's face.

"I see." She walked back to the door and opened it slowly. "Well, I am sorry you had to deal with that. Just give him some time. He will come around," She said the words over her shoulder as she exited the room. I hated the position it put her in. A woman shouldn't have to choose between her son and her husband, but how dare he put this all on me. Sleep. That's what I needed. This long work week had been trying. I had other things to worry about than the approval of an old angry man.

As I lay in bed on top of the black satin sheets, I thought, *Surely tomorrow will be better.* My date with Claire was a definite pick me up, and the thought of being busy all weekend was an even bigger bonus as it would keep me out of the house and away from him.

I returned to work the next morning and a steaming cup of black coffee sat on my desk next to a stress ball. *Beth!*

By lunchtime, I had met with all the vendors, and I had spent the better part of the afternoon preparing the report for the board meeting. This was the first time since I graduated that I had actually done something I could be proud of. I regretted slacking for the last few years. I was a natural in the business field.

This morning I had received a strange new message from a girl named Lola. I didn't remember seeing her, and upon reading her profile, I was . . . disturbed. She was very into heavy metal and the color black. She put in her profile that she liked going to raves and "rocking out." I was impressed with her love of poetry, which I didn't share as an interest, but the way she was able to respond to the questions using the poetry was intriguing. When asked what kind of man she wanted, she responded with, "The type of man with an open mind, a heart of steel, and knows how to unwind!"

Weird, right? Kind of cool but still weird. Her bleached blonde hair was striped with black, and her dark brown eyes stared straight through you. However, she was wearing a corset type top that was insanely hot. I argued with myself about whether or not we could make this work. I couldn't imagine my parents' faces when they met her, but maybe the profile wasn't really representing her appearance. *Catfish?* There was photo shop and all kinds of ways to change a picture. The message was more of a flyer for a rave party next Thursday night at an abandoned warehouse downtown that had been converted to a club of sorts. I had heard of it but never got the courage to go, and Camille wouldn't have been caught dead at a place like that.

I had responded to her message saying I'd be there and asked how I would find her. I was still feeling a bit off about her, but who knew, maybe she'd steal my heart with one of her poems. Okay maybe not, but I had no doubt it would be an experience I wouldn't forget.

FIVE

THIS IDEA OF MEETING these girls whenever they messaged me was starting to get out of hand. I had dates coming out of my ears and with my job bearing down on me, I was busy. Maybe too busy. Jenna had requested my appearance Saturday morning at ten and said we would be "busy" most of the day. I was totally scared of what that might mean. Hell, she'd probably have me dropping from a cliff or something.

Claire's last message said, "I know we live far apart so can we meet at the mall downtown and drive from there? I was thinking around eight?" *Sweet.*

And then there was Victoria, she had not set up a date, but we had messaged a few times a day about random stuff like what my thoughts on kids were and what kind of movies I liked. I figured that she hadn't had time to meet me with her two job work schedule during the day, and I respected her not wanting to meet me with a kid around.

"Mr. Sloane, your father would like to meet with you." Beth had once again poked her head in without me noticing.

"Sure thing," I said, sliding back from my desk. "And thanks for the coffee and this," I said holding up the stress ball. Beth smiled and left. Usually she just turned and left. I wondered if my new project was earning me some kind of respect in the company or maybe it was our mutual commiseration about dealing with my father. I made a mental note to talk to her later about some of my ideas. I knew she was my father's "right hand man" and her input would be helpful, and I didn't happen to mind her smile to brighten my day.

I entered my father's office with my hands shoved in my pockets. "Yes, father, you wanted to see me."

He was staring out the window watching a plane take off from our private runway. He turned around, greeting me with a smile. "Son, I have been hearing good things about your evaluations. I hope you will be ready to present your results at the meeting on Tuesday." I had not seen him smile for anyone except my mother in a long time. I hadn't realized how much his approval meant since I graduated high school and didn't become a pilot or a meteorologist, even though I was pretty sure my mother had threatened him to stop fighting with me.

"Uh yeah, I am finishing up the proposal, and the last vendor is coming this afternoon. The project will be ready for approval Tuesday."

"Marvelous! Your mother will be attending the meeting as well. She has also requested you come to lunch on Sunday, if you are available?"

I agreed. Mom's Sunday lunches were always good, and it had been a while since we had done anything as a family. I knew being the only child and not wanting to follow in the family footsteps was disappointing enough for my father.

I had to rush out to meet the vendor about a new badge system. Several of the employees had complained that our security system was outdated. Right now they had to access a computer at the front entrance to type in their credentials and clock in to get in or out. I agreed that was a bit much especially if you were running low on time or your hands were full. This person had offered several solutions including an eye scanner, an encrypted badge, and a voice recognition system. I had him price the first two only because he had advised the voice system could be an issue if there was background noise, like a plane taking off for instance.

At five o'clock sharp I headed out the door. I was excited to meet Claire. But as I pulled into my driveway my phone went off. A text message came through from Claire. It read, "Hey Drew! It's Claire. I am sorry, but I got called in to work tonight. I'm not bailing, but it might be a little later than eight. Do you think you could meet me here at the hotel around nine? I'll understand if you can't, just let me know."

I told her that would be fine. I did wonder how it would work if we were together? Would she be working all the time; all night or all weekend? Would we have to work around her schedule more often than not?

I pulled my car up to the front entrance of the Raleigh Manor Inn a few hours later. The motor rumbled noisily under the covered drop off area, and the valet who didn't look a day over eighteen ran up to take the wheel. "Oh man, this is a nice ride!"

I remembered feeling that same way when I saw it for sale on the side of the road about five years ago. I had paid cash for it that day, and it had been roaring like a lion ever since. "Yeah kid, just take care of it!"

"No problem, sir." I heard the door shut and the engine boom as he put it into gear.

I checked the collar on my black polo shirt and smoothed my hair down one last time before I entered the large glass entryway. A line of people waiting to be seated stretched all the way to the door. I quickly bypassed the line not wanting to be late meeting Claire. I wasn't after all waiting to be seated. I crossed the room to the double doors leading into the dining room where I waited for a few moments before seeing a tall, thin man wearing a tailored black suit approaching me. He quietly said, "Can I help you, sir?"

"Yes, I am here to see Claire. She's expecting me."

"Right this way." The elderly man seemed tired beyond his years. He walked with a slight limp in his left foot. Leading me through the double doors and into the kitchen, he directed me to sit at a side table to wait. I figured it was used as a break table for the kitchen staff.

The kitchen smelled amazing. I could smell the garlic and the wine simmering. Even the steam from the vegetables permeated the room. There were trays of food waiting on a heated counter to be picked up by the waiters sprinting to and from the room. The kitchen was noisy. The pots and pans clanked together, and I could hear a wire whisk briskly moving in a metal bowl. I hadn't seen anyone come out of the kitchen, but the old waiter had poked his head in and motioned for someone to let them know I was here. A young female cook came out carrying a steaming plate of mussels and a glass of white wine.

"Compliments of the chef," she said with a wink. I thanked her, and she scurried off into the kitchen. I could hear her squealing inside and that boosted my confidence a little. Hopefully Claire was that excited to see me.

I was starving so I quickly downed the first few mussels. They were fantastic, served with a side of potato gnocchi in a delicious mushroom sauce. I sipped the wine which paired nicely with the hearty broth. The warm liquid felt good going down my parched throat.

By the time I finished my plate, another dish was brought out, this time carried by another female staff member. This woman was older, and her sly grin clued me in on the chatter going on inside the kitchen.

"The chef should be done soon, but there are a few courses left for you to taste."

"Please give my regards to the chef, the dishes are fantastic." I tried to boost my voice, which sparked a giggle from behind the door. The older chef smiled and gave a slight bow before reentering through those mysterious kitchen doors.

The second course was a roasted duck breast sliced thinly over a bed of wild rice served with steamed green beans, which were seasoned nicely with garlic and sea salt. I couldn't remember the last time I had duck, but I was almost certain it had not been this good. A man could get use to this kind of cooking.

I didn't mind sitting alone in this hallway table. The bustle from the kitchen was quite relaxing and being able to enjoy my food without the prying eyes of other patrons gave me a chance to savor the dishes.

I leaned back in my chair and sipped the remaining wine from my glass. A few of the other kitchen staff were beginning to leave and the door opened and shut a million times before I saw her. And I can honestly say it was worth the wait. She entered through the doors still wearing her apron over a light pink long sleeved blouse and a pair of jeans. Her chocolate brown hair was up in a tight bun, and she was void of any makeup. She was lovely.

In her hands were two bowls of chocolate mousse with a strawberry glaze and a few sugared strawberries with a mint leaf for garnish. Top notch from what I could see. I was very impressed with her menu tonight. I stood as she approached the table. She set down the dishes and removed her apron. I saw a quick flash of blonde hair cover the circle window in the door, but she flitted away.

"Hi, I'm Drew. It is so nice to meet you. And you're food is amazing. Really, just spectacular." I was rambling. I reached to shake her hand, and she graciously reached for mine.

"I am so sorry about tonight! My chef got sick, and the manager begged me to come back. It was a mess, and Fridays are our biggest night." She flipped a stray piece of hair off her forehead.

"No, really, it is totally fine," I said. "I have sincerely enjoyed my time just interacting with your staff and tasting your delicious food. May I?" I said motioning towards the chocolaty dish in front of me.

"Of course," she said. She reached for her bowl as well, and we both dug in.

"Mmmm! That is insane." I meant it. That shit was amazing.

"Ya know, after cooking all night you would think I would get tired of the food, but I try to put things on the menu that you can't resist." She dug her spoon deeper into the fluffy mousse and brought it to her mouth. She slowly licked the spoon, which I found incredibly sexy.

We finished the dessert, and I offered to walk her out. It was almost eleven by the time we made our way to the parking lot. I was exhausted from the day's work, and she was yawning the whole way out the door.

"I want to make it up to you. I know this was a lousy first date," she said.

"Not at all. In fact I actually enjoyed myself, but I would be interested in seeing you again soon. Is your schedule pretty flexible?"

"Umm, I work a lot on the weekends, but I am off most mornings. I am technically off on Sundays, but something always seems to happen. I haven't had much need for a social life, so I put a lot of hours in at work. What about Sunday though? I am sure I can work something out." She sounded like she was trying. It did bother me that she would have to change around her life just to spend time with me, but from what I could tell she was a nice person.

I agreed to dinner on Sunday night, not in her hotel, and we parted ways with a quick hug. I had noticed that she smelled my shirt when we embraced; when she stepped back, she looked slightly intoxicated. Silently thanking the makers of Axe Body Spray I held out a steadying hand. "It was so nice to meet you, Claire." I wondered how long it had been since she was close to a man.

She got in a modest sedan, a Toyota maybe, and drove out of sight. The valet attendant drove up and thanked me again for bringing such a cool car.

I wasn't sad that the night was ending. The date had gone well, and I was eager to get some sleep. Jenna had texted confirming we were to meet at ten the next morning, and to quote her text I needed to "bring something I could get wet in."

The beach maybe?

I had no idea what this girl was thinking, and I was so tired at the moment, I didn't care. I stripped down to my boxers and passed out in between the silk sheets as soon as my head touched the pillow.

SIX

MORNING CAME TOO early as I had predicted the night before. I woke up around eight thirty, and I rushed to quickly shower and shave before slipping on some cargo shorts and a tight, blue T-shirt. I threw some swimming trunks and a tank top in a bag and headed out the door. I didn't want her to come here, so we were meeting at her fitness studio before heading to our destination.

When I pulled up a few minutes early, I could see right into the room where Jenna was teaching a yoga seminar. I had to turn my head sideways to figure out where her legs began and ended. I doubted my eyes could get any bigger looking at the toned muscles and shapely flesh.

The day was already steaming hot and watching her was about to fog up the windows. I didn't have to wait long for her to come jogging out of the building.

"Hey there, handsome! You 'bout ready to join me for an adventure?" She was so vibrant and full of life, that her energy was contagious.

"Well yes, ma'am. Where are we headed this fine summer day?" I said in my best cowboy impression. She laughed and put her bag in the car. I was happy that she hadn't changed her outfit because she was scorching hot in the tight black ensemble.

"You will just have to wait and see." She smiled, laying her phone on the dashboard. I heard the mysterious female voice telling me to exit the parking lot and turn right. How cool was it that she came prepared with preprogrammed directions. The mystery behind her date was equally exhilarating and terrifying at the same time. Who knew where we were headed? I turned the car around and headed down the road. The system said that we were about an hour and a half away from our destination. The conversation flowed until a song came on that I hadn't heard in forever. It was an older song from that movie *Grease* called *Summer Days* or *Summer Nights*.

"May I?" she said.

I motioned to the radio and said, "Feel free." She cranked it up and started dancing with her hands in the air and singing with a less than *American Idol* voice, but she was hilarious. She had me cracking up the whole way there—wherever there was.

I began to see some signs as we got off the interstate for a water park. I had never been there, but the commercials were all over the TV during the summer. They boasted mile high water slides and a million gallon wave pool. I was excited about trying something new, but I had an eerie feeling that I was about to face some kind of fear.

I looked over at Jenna right after we passed the umpteenth sign, and she sucked in her lips like she was hiding a secret and tried to turn away from me. I reached over and rubbed the side of her chin, and she busted out laughing.

"What's so funny?" I asked.

She just shook her head smiling and said, "You'll see!"

As we approached the water park, the smile got bigger, and I started to get excited about playing in the water with Jenna. We parked about a mile from the entrance in the only parking spot left and grabbed our stuff to head inside. The line to enter the park was long as well, but we made light of the time by talking and joking about the slides that we could see. Jenna was challenging me to ride every ride in the park, and had I had any idea what they were like, I wouldn't have accepted.

As soon as we were through the gates, we went to the bathrooms to change. I popped out first wearing my navy blue Ralph Lauren trunks, and I was anxious to see what she was wearing. It didn't disappoint.

"Holy shit," I mumbled when she came bounding out of the dressing room wearing a red polka dot itty-bitty bikini.

"What's that?" she said.

I had to recover, but it wasn't easy. I struggled to find a way to tell her how bad I'd like to take her home instead of down an above the clouds water slide. "I said holy shit, you look amazing." *Nice, Drew. Nice recovery.* Thank God she didn't slap me; instead she did a little pose showing off the smooth, tanned, toned . . . well, you get the picture.

What happened next was a blur of chlorinated water and scorching hot sun. I was having a great time. A few rides required we sit together on an inner tube. I won't lie that when she slid into my lap and we headed down the slope, I had to think of everything but the way her body felt so close to mine.

She knew it too. She would snuggle deeply back into my arms and scream like she was scared even when I knew she wasn't. I didn't mind though. She felt good there.

It wasn't until we reached the towering slope of the tallest slide on the East Coast that I realized this is why she brought me. I watched from the bottom as someone risked their life for an eight second thrill. I could hear the plastic creaking to support the weight of the gallons of water, and I could see the water pouring out of the leaks, which led any sane man to believe the structure was not sound. "Nah, I don't think so, Jenna. How about I catch you?" She shook her head no, which sent her long hair slinging in different directions. "I mean look at that thing, it's practically falling apart."

"Come on, Drew. It will be great, and if you don't like it, there is another slide half way up that is covered. At least walk me up." That sounded reasonable. She took my hand and dragged me to the thirteen-story stair-case.

I reluctantly followed her stair by stair enjoying the view on the way. She kept a tight grip on my hand like she was trying to keep me from running away. But that kept her tight body right in front of my face the whole way. For a moment, I forgot what we were doing. In hindsight, I bet that was what she wanted. I know I'm a sucker.

I didn't even notice I was a million miles off the ground until we hit the line at the top. Only three people stood between me and death. I wasn't about to dive to my doom today.

"Okay, well, have a good time. I'll see you at the bottom." I waved and started back down the stairs.

"Oh don't be such a baby, Drew! Even little girls go down this slide. Are you wimpier than a little girl, Drew?" I heard giggles from all the people hanging around the rails getting ready to go down. A line was forming behind us, and a girl that was maybe eleven years old pushed past me to get to the slide.

"See!" she said. "Don't be a little girl, Drew." I didn't appreciate the taunts, but with loads of people watching our interaction, I had no choice.

I sat down on the slide and closed my eyes. The lifeguard started to say something, and I grasped onto the rails stalling every second I could. The water was freezing cold and even though the heat was sweltering today, the cold water only exasperated the chills running up my spine.

"Okay, so you want to lie completely back and . . ." The lifeguard was cut off by Jenna approaching me quickly from behind. I wasn't exactly ready when she gave me a push, if you could call sending me airborne off a thirteen-story death trap a push. I went flying off the edge and down the rushing waters all the way down to the heaping pool of water at the bottom. I felt sharp pain rushing through my body as I came to a stop. My stomach churned sharply, and I felt my heart rise up in my throat. I could barely breathe, much less stand. No longer was I worried about dying, but

I was pretty sure I broke something from the pain swirling in my stomach. I heard shouts coming from the tower, which was surely Jenna.

"Hey man, are you okay?" It was a lifeguard, but I could only hear the ringing in my ears. I pushed myself up and out of the splash zone, limping to the bench across the way. I heard the rushing water and the splash as another rider came flying through. The lifeguard had followed me over to make sure I was okay. "You are supposed to cross your legs and arms before you go down, if not the rush at the bottom hits you right in the nads, man."

"Yeah, thanks for the advice, after I came down." I was none too pleased with the lack of information.

"Yikes, dude! They are supposed to tell you up top . . ." his words traveled off as Jenna crossed the sidewalk to get to me.

"Yeah, maybe if I hadn't been pushed early then I could have heard the instructions." I smoothed out my shorts trying to adjust some of the pressure and pain.

"Aww, did you get hurt?" she said in a baby voice. She reached her arm around my shoulder and kissed my cheek.

I was furious, beyond words. She rubbed my shoulder, and I laid my head back on the bench. I was starting to feel dehydrated and sun burnt. I wanted to leave. I got off the bench and turned around to face her. I wanted to find a way to say nicely that I was ready to head out. Apparently the park didn't close until eleven and it was only four, so another seven hours of gut wrenching pain did not sound pleasant.

"Hey, I am kind of hungry. Are you ready to get out of here?" I stretched one arm behind my head to scratch my neck.

She seemed to take the hint and rose off the bench. We walked arm in arm to the gate passing one last ride. I felt the tug on my arm, and I knew she was hinting that we try the "slingshot." I know, right? The name alone tells you that it's not a good idea. They strap you into a seat and literally slingshot you into the air. "No way," I muttered, tugging her in the other direction. Thankfully, she didn't even ask. I was trying get over the feeling of resentment generating in me. I mean, other than the water hammer to my nuts, I had lived. But could I handle being taunted or pushed every time she wanted me to do something I wasn't comfortable with?

We headed to a local steakhouse, which gave me a chance to cool off. By the time we were seated I was relaxed again. She had been on edge too, and I hated feeling like jerk. "Hey Jen, I am sorry about earlier. I was just in a lot of, umm, pain," I said, readjusting my pants.

She reached for my hand and squeezed it. "No, I'm sorry. I can get carried away sometimes. I'm a jerk, sorry." She seemed genuine and that further eased my fears.

She bit into her garden panini, and I cut up my twelve ounce steak. The conversation began to flow again, and she told me about all her adventures and what she still wanted to do. She asked about what I wanted to do, and honestly, it was none of the same things.

I wanted to travel, preferably by train or car, to visit landmarks and museums, and she wanted to jump out of planes and deep-sea dive. She still seemed interested in what I wanted, but I was still worried about whether she would be happy if I only *supported* her in her adventures but did not *accompany* her on them.

We drove home right as the sun was setting. We had the windows down, blasting country music. She was singing along with her feet hanging out the window. She laid her head on my arm, and I quickly wrapped my arm around her.

The drive home went surprisingly fast, so when we pulled up at her studio I didn't really know how to end the night. Turning into the parking lot of her yoga studio, I slid the car into an empty space near the back. The parking lot was still bustling, even after dark people were entering the gym in crowds. I turned to my beautiful passenger and said, "Thanks for the trip, I had a good time. And you looked amazing in that swimsuit." I flashed a wide grin not able to hide my excitement.

"Yeah." She smiled. "You said that a few times" She was still holding tightly to my arm when she laid a long lingering kiss on me. She splayed her fingers on my neck and gently pulled herself over the shifter and onto my lap.

She tasted like the mint-flavored gum she had popped in her mouth a few minutes before, and I had no doubt that she had planned all this from the moment she got in the car. I liked it, but I wondered if under that adventurous carefree attitude, if she didn't have some sort of motive behind it all.

Maybe I was just looking for reasons to doubt her. After all, she didn't know about my money or my parents company, so what did she stand to gain? I had planned to tell the girls more about who I was after our third date *if* we managed to make it for three dates.

I snapped out of my thoughts and realized that we had stopped kissing. She had moved down my neck and was slipping her hands under my shirt. She hadn't taken the time to change fully; she had only put on a short bright red cloth cover-up shirt instead.

I ran my hand up one smooth silky thigh, and she moaned into my throat. She was arching her back and moving her hips over my jeans, and I grew tense. It's not like I didn't want her because I did, but I wasn't feeling it with her. She was gorgeous and sexy, but something was off, and I wasn't ready to take this on in a crowded parking lot where she worked. Sounds ridiculous, right?

She leaned back and lifted up her cover up and the goods that came spilling out just about changed my mind.

Jenna smiled as I admired her perfect body. My hands slid up the inside of her thighs. This chick had more toned lean muscle than I had ever encountered, and there was a part of me, a growing part of me, that wanted to see how tight she could squeeze. Jenna reached down for my pants, and I almost let it happen.

"Jenna, wait." I wanted to kick myself for what I was about to do. I could only see the shadows walking by the car as the windows had already fogged up. It wasn't exactly a mystery as to what was happening. Jenna leaned back against the steering wheel and gave me a confused look.

"What's wrong?" she said. Her voice was so raspy, and she was still breathing hard from the adrenaline.

"I don't have any protection." It was the first thing that came to my mind. It was also a lie, but she didn't need to know that.

She looked pissed. "Okay then." She climbed off my lap leaving me with a sudden chill. She grabbed her stuff and reached for the door. "So I guess I'll see you later." I could see her eyes roll from the other side of the car, and it was really annoying.

"Whoa there! What's wrong?" I had made up my mind up already, but I needed this confirmation.

"I don't know. I thought we were having a good time and now you are just blowing me off?" Her frustration showed in her posture and her attitude. "You know what, it's whatever. I don't have time to *talk* you into to having a good time." The way she emphasized the 'talk' part sounded like she was referring to my fear of heights. Big mistake!

"All right, well, have a nice day." I started the car and put it into gear. She huffed once more before storming out of the car and slamming the door shut.

"Wow, maybe they should teach anger management with the yoga classes," I said to myself as I spun the wheel leaving the parking lot.

"Next!"

SEVEN

I WAS NOT A FAN OF early mornings, but being up to go to work every morning had ruined my ability to sleep in. *Thanks Dad!* My parents were expecting me for lunch this fine Sunday morning.

My mom loved making lunch on Sundays for whoever might show up. The menu was always divine, and I was looking forward to a home cooked meal. It's not like I had a long drive to get to the dinner table, I did live in the same house. The reason for the invitation was that for the last nine Sundays I had other plans with Camille. She always planned for us to be out of town exploring the country on weekends, which is another reason I couldn't make it to work on time most days. I was recovering from the boozy all-nighters.

I came down to lunch wearing a pair of cargo shorts and a tank top. The meal she was already working on smelled delicious. The house smelled like lemon and blueberry.

I rounded the corner to the dining room, and I could hear voices. I stopped for a moment to listen. "Mrs. Sloane, is there anything I can help you with?" The voice sounded familiar, but I couldn't quite place it.

"No dear, but thank you. Why don't you have a seat and tell me how things are at the office?" My mother's sugary sweet voice had a hint of curiosity in it. I stood waiting in the hall, skimming the conversation to see whom it was and if my name would come up. Okay, I was eavesdropping.

"Actually it is all going very smoothly. The employee evaluations are being handled by Drew, and from what I have heard, he has been very thorough." She sounded impressed, whoever she was. I stood there like a little schoolgirl grinning over my success. "He has even covered some of the more *personal* issues with the ladies' room." She let out a small giggle.

"Is that so?" my mother responded. "Andrew has always been very diplomatic. I am pleased to see that he has found his niche. I will be there for the meeting on Tuesday, and I look forward to seeing his presentation." *Thanks, Mom, no pressure.* I heard footsteps coming, and I couldn't risk being caught listening.

I rounded the corner and greeted my mother. "Mom, this smells amazing!" I couldn't see our guest's face, but from the back I saw shoulder length dirty blonde hair hanging over lightly tanned smooth skin. She had a small frame, and she was wearing a flowing summer dress with a floral print rippling along the layers. Her tiny feet donned flip-flop style shoes that complemented her long legs. Very feminine. I tried to picture who in our office looked like that, but I fell flat. Most of our staff wore colorless suits and heels.

"Andrew! Thank you for coming. Will you grab that cake out of the oven for me?"

"Putting me to work already, huh?" I joked. My mother was nothing like my father's cold exterior. She was happy to move out of the business world and explore other hobbies like cooking and dinner parties. I chanced a look at our guest from my new angle, and I was stunned.

Beth! She didn't look the same out of her white collared shirts and ponytail attire. I don't believe I had ever noticed how beautiful she was. I stood staring for a moment before she shyly looked away. I went back to retrieving the cake out of the oven.

"Andrew, Beth and I were just talking about how well you have done with this project," my mother prodded.

"Oh?" I arched my eyebrows in Beth's direction. She gave me a half-cocked smile and turned her attention to my mother.

"Yes, she was telling me what a wonderful job you are doing. I very much am looking forward to seeing your presentation. Are you finished with it?"

That was my mother's version of checking up on me. She never out-right asked, but she was the master of beating around the bush to get to the point. "Yes, actually I completed it on Friday. There are a few points to cover, and I plan to fine tune it all on Monday." I gave her a few moments to let it sink in, and I moved on to the next non-work related topic. "What is this delicious cake?"

"Oh! I saw a new recipe on one of those food shows. It's a lemon pound cake, and I have a fresh blueberry sauce to go on it."

"Damn, that sounds good."

"Andrew! Language!" my mother hissed. Beth let out a giggle, and I shrugged off the lashing. I let the hot vapors stream into my nostrils, dying to taste it, but my mother would have my head if I touched it before dessert.

I snooped around in the kitchen trying to find out what else we were having. I could see some kind of fish with nuts on it roasting in the oven, and of course macaroni salad was in the fridge.

My mom set some cups and silverware on the counter behind me. "Son, can you and Beth go set the table for me; the table on the sunporch preferably? It's a beautiful day out."

I grabbed the plates, and Beth stood to get the napkins and silverware. We walked to the sun porch in silence with only the sticky flop of her shoes and the silverware clanging together.

We entered the all glass sunporch, and I put the off-white china on the neatly made table. My mother changed the table decorations weekly, and this time she had small purple tea light candles surrounding a bouquet of brightly colored summer flowers. Beth started neatly folding the napkins, and I spread out the plates and cups at each setting. The sun was blaring in on one side of the room, and I immediately went to shut the shades.

"Does your mother do this every Sunday?"

"Yeah actually. It is kind of her *thing* now that she doesn't come to the office as much." I busied myself at the table. She only had four place settings, and I knew my dad would be down eventually. *Great.*

"I meant what I told your mom. I think you are doing a wonderful job." Her voice was sweet, and it was definitely a change not to hear her ordering me around. I nodded and she kept going. "I saw some of those requests, and well they are pretty out there. I couldn't imagine *you* being up for that."

"What do you mean?" I said, sounding more defensive than necessary.

"Well, just some of those things seemed . . . personal." Her cheeks had flushed as she mindlessly adjusted a set of silverware next to the gold-rimmed colored plates.

"I like to think that I can be objective and serious when the time calls for it." I didn't know whether she was insulting me or trying to flatter me. I decided to give her the benefit of the doubt in the name of hospitality today. I didn't like seeing her squirm over her doubt of my character. Besides, I hadn't given her much reason to have faith in my work until now.

My mother broke the awkwardness when she brought in the steaming hot fish fillet and set it on the table. "Would you two mind helping me bring the other dishes?" Beth scurried back to the kitchen before I even had a chance to respond.

I jogged back into the kitchen and tried to make peace over the conversation. "Look, I get it. I have been a jerk at work. I guess I didn't see how important my role in the company is so, yeah, I am trying to turn all that around." I leaned forward on the counter, and she turned to face me. "Thank you for noticing."

"Everyone has noticed a change in you." She crossed her arms and continued her evaluation. "Your father is really happy about that."

My automated smile dimmed as soon as the look on my father's face at lunch the other day flashed through my mind. I had hoped he would take it serious, but I probably didn't deserve anyone's praise, not yet at least. We grabbed the trays and headed back to the porch where my parents seated at the table.

"Beth! It's a pleasure to see you. Thank you for coming." The old man smiled with real happiness before turning to me. "I am glad you could make it the whole two hundred feet over here, son." His voice held more sarcasm than I'd like to hear, but I brushed it off for my mother's sake.

"Oh Wyatt, hush up. Don't go running him off when he is finally here," my mother scolded him.

"Dear, I was just saying that the boy could make it over more often, he just lives next door." My dad shrugged his shoulders and started serving himself with the meal.

It took everything I had not to get up and leave. He always managed to find a way to embarrass me in front of company. He couldn't pass up the opportunity to say how his poor, useless son could never make it to lunch. I was more embarrassed that Beth had to hear this nonsense, especially when she was looking so beautiful at the table seated across from me.

My father tried to talk about work, but my mother quickly hushed him in favor of learning more about his assistant—his very beautiful assistant.

"Beth, are you from this area?" *Good call, Mom.* I wanted to know that answer as well.

She spilled quite a few details that I hadn't known. She was originally from Maine, which struck me as odd. She talked about how much better the weather was here and that when her parents had moved to the beach in Florida, she had decided to move south as well. Beth said that her parents were both in the weather related industry. Her mom was a meteorologist for a TV station, and her dad had run a Search and Rescue team with the Coast Guard. Beth was from a small town and said that she was happy to be out of there.

Her eyes seemed relieved when she said that, and I wondered what else might have gone on prior to her leaving.

"Do you fly much?" my mother asked.

"Not unless I have to. I've seen too many bad endings to flights."

My mother and father both laughed at her confession. "Well, Andrew down there is afraid of heights. How odd is it that you both work for a company that does nothing but fly people from place to place?"

They continued laughing, and Beth and I sat looking at each other. I shrugged and said, "That just goes to show you how good we are at our jobs." I winked at her.

She reached for her goblet of freshly squeezed lemonade and took a big gulp. My mother slid her chair back and excused herself from the table. She was only gone for a moment before she returned with dessert. "My goodness, Mother, this looks incredible." In her hand was a perfect loaf of the lemon pound cake with gooey blueberry sauce dripping down the sides. We all oohed and ahhed over the dessert, and I wasn't shy when I sliced off a huge piece for myself.

I watched as Beth took her first bite. She locked her lips over the bite and slid the fork out of her mouth before closing her eyes and massaging the food in her mouth. It was sort of a fetish of mine to watch someone taste something that I knew was good. Not like a freaky fetish, but it did give me some insight to their personality. My mind roamed to what else she might have that reaction towards.

Damn, I had to get this search under control. I had already *"test drove"* some new people, and from what I could tell I was beginning to be too picky for my own good. I still didn't know what or whom I wanted. Thankfully so far I had been able to control this task to what my brain was thinking instead of what my body was feeling.

After lunch was over, Beth and I offered to clear the table and join my parents on the patio for cocktails. We made a pretty good team. I scraped the food into the trash, and she stacked the plates in the dishwasher. We boxed up the leftovers and cleaned up around the kitchen. We didn't really speak, but I did *accidentally* bump into her a time or two.

This different side of Beth was very attractive. She seemed to be unimpressed with my money or stature, which was a good thing I guess. I wasn't sure how she felt about me to be honest. Maybe she didn't feel anything.

I grabbed a beer out of the fridge, and we headed outside. The day was beautiful, and the sun beating down on the glistening pool was like an invitation to go for a swim. I took off my shirt and sat down at the table where my parents were talking about going to the Bahamas. I knew they wouldn't. My father never left the company for more than a day or so. It bugged the hell out of my mom that he didn't spend more time with her.

"It is sweltering out here," Beth said, fanning herself with her hand. "I wish I had brought my bathing suit." She laughed, but the idea had crossed my mind several times already to get her into a swimsuit.

"Actually, darling, we have a few swimsuits that might fit you. We had bought them for our niece, but she hasn't been by to use them.

Beth sucked in a deep breath. It was obvious she was just making conversation, but you couldn't say "no" to my parents' hospitality.

"Yeah, I will show you where they are. I would like to take a swim myself." I stood and motioned to the pool house across the pool. She lifted her eyebrows and slowly stood. Mother headed back inside to get another pitcher of sangria, and we headed off to change.

The pool was beautifully decorated with plants and trees lining the walkways. The palms leaned over the pool creating a nice area of shade from the beating sun. The pool house wasn't huge, but trying to move around the floats and lawn chairs was tricky. I reached into the cabinet housing the swimsuits and grabbed a few for her to choose from. I was instantly excited to see the options. One was a black two-piece with silver pieces linking the top together. Another was a beach scene string bikini in a sunset color pallet. The last was an olive green halter-top bikini. I could see her smooth tan skin in that one the best. I held it up, and she reluctantly grabbed it. We stood in the steamy room standing face to face. She looked kind of shaken up. She was much shorter than my towering six foot two frame. Her face only came up to my shoulders. I could picture her laying her head down on my chest and me wrapping my arms around her.

"Are you going to give me the room to change?" Her words slashed through my little fantasy like a knife, and I quickly turned to leave the room. If she were a different woman, any other woman for that matter, I would have laid a kiss on her that would have left us both spinning, but she was different.

Untouchable.

I stood so long trying to replay the whole encounter in my head that she beat me out of the dressing room. I slid the trunks on and hurried out the door in time to see her dive off the diving board and into the cool blue water. Without shoes the concrete burned into my feet so I hurried over to the board and stood waiting for her to surface. I could see her lean body shimmering through the bottom of the pool, and when she came up for air, she was all the way across the pool.

I dove into the freezing cold water and made my way to her on the other side. The water felt so good on my sun burnt skin. I opened my eyes underwater, and I could see her getting closer. I resurfaced inches from her face, and she squealed, "Oh my gosh!"

"Sorry," I said, rubbing the water off my face. She dipped lower in the pool and drenched her hair in water. I didn't step back and neither did she. "This feels so good," I said.

"Yeah, I needed to cool off . . . from the sun I mean." She turned around to look back at my parents. When she saw their eyes on us, I knew the moment was over. She waded to a shady spot on the edge of the pool and started talking to my parents about how nice the water felt. My mother offered her another glass of wine, and she willingly accepted it. I dunked my head under water, and my eyes resurfaced with the heavenly sight of Beth coming out of the pool. The olive green bikini clung to her curves, and her hair slipped over her shoulder revealing a very tan, very smooth back. So many dirty thoughts ran through my mind.

Beth hurried back to the water to escape the burning cement with two glasses of wine. The sweet liquid went down easy. I tried to pull off a toast, "To a hot day and a cool pool." But she responded with an eye roll and continued to sip her beverage.

Okay, I get it. She didn't really know me. All I am is the boss's lazy son, but I could be different. Hell, I was already changing, and maybe if I could show her, I might actually interest her.

Beth gulped down her drink and set the glass on the side of the pool. She made one last trip to the diving board, and I watched her gracefully dive in. She swam underwater to the other side of the pool and exited without so much as another glance at me. I covered my chest with my hand signaling the sharp knife had penetrated my chest, but she continued to walk in the opposite direction towards the shack housing her clothes. I could see through one of the windows as she dried her hair with a towel and patted the soft cloth on her shoulders and face.

Her eyes darted over to me, and once again I was busted. What can I say? I am not the type to hide my attempts to *woo* a woman. I want whomever I am with to feel like she is the only one I could be staring at. Beth, however, glared at me like some peeping Tom and shut the wooden blinds blocking out any view. It wasn't like I was watching her change.

Rejected! Nice, Drew. My losing streak was starting to get to me.

I hopped out of the pool and went over to my parents' table carrying the empty glasses with me. The water dripping off my arms splattered onto the table as I reached for the picture of wine. "Honestly Andrew, have you no manners? You couldn't have changed before showering us with your pool water?"

I reached for a handful of the chips and salsa my parents were sharing and said, "Beth is in there right now. Not like we can both change at the same time."

"That's right," my father said sternly. "Beth is a *very* nice girl and a hard worker. Don't you go messing that up." He snapped the newspaper back open and disappeared behind the gray shield.

"And how would I do that, Father?" I knew what he was thinking already, but my father had a way of spinning things that had happened in my life into something I caused instead of something I had to work through.

"Boys, I won't have you fighting in front of company," my mom said in a stern voice, cloaked in a wide smile she was flashing to our guest. Beth was coming out of the pool house in her beautiful sundress. Her wet hair crinkled into loose curls, and I wondered if that was her natural hair type.

"Beth, will you be joining us for dinner? We are so happy to have you here." My mother swooned over our guest. I would love to be able to say that my mother's sugary sweet personality was fake and that I didn't constantly roll my eyes when she spoke, but that wasn't the case. My mother was the most perky, loving person I had ever met, which must be why I am so irresistible. *Okay.* Well, I thought I was until I met this assortment of women who kept resisting my charm.

That daunting reality smacked me in the face like a sledgehammer every time my eyes met with the unimpressed, uninterested Beth. *You know what that meant? Challenge accepted.*

EIGHT

AFTER BETH HAD turned down my mother's dinner proposal and politely left the premises, I realized my date with Claire was this evening, if she managed to clear her schedule. I sent a text message to find out where and if we would be seeing each other this evening.

Claire responded, "Yes, I am free for dinner tonight. I was wondering how you'd feel about coming to my place for dinner? I have a few recipes I want to test on you. ;)"

The winking smiley face at the end hit the mark. My thoughts had been diving deep into the gutter thinking about all the things I'd like her to test on me. "Sounds great! Just send me the address and what time you want me there." The words in my head sounded so different from the words I quickly swiped on the screen.

She sent me the address and said eight thirty, which gave me some time to chill for a minute before I finished getting ready. "What to wear to her house?" I said aloud. My closet was full of suits and dressy clothes, but this was just to hang out and eat some, probably amazing, food.

I settled on jeans and a gray fitted T-shirt from Abercrombie. I checked myself out in the mirror a few times, before deciding that, "Yeah, I look good!"

I bounded down the stairs and out the side entrance hoping to escape any further questioning by my parents. My father hadn't let the fact that I had obviously found his secretary attractive and that I was bound to screw up a good thing for the company. *Thanks Dad!*

When I arrived at Claire's apartment building, I found it a little sketchy. The neighborhood was really quiet, void of street lights or any lights for that matter. There was an eerie glow coming from the building's entrance. I almost developed a fear of the dark just sitting in my car deciding whether or not to get out. I began to wonder if the power was out. I checked the address again and it was exactly right.

Jenna's daunting words echoed in my head, "Don't be such a girl, Drew." I argued over whether this was a valid fear, before saying out loud, "Maybe she shouldn't live in such a creepy neighborhood."

It was time to man up, so I got out of the car fully ready to run like a little girl into the building if I saw anything creepy. But I managed to make it to the door without incident, and Claire was waiting at the top of the stairs when I burst through the doors.

She was wearing a navy blue wrap dress that landed about knee length. It was very simple but elegant, and her black flat shoes hinted that her profession made her very aware of her comfort levels. Claire's hair was hanging in loose curly locks around her shoulders. The front was pushed back with a pin. She looked comfortable.

"I was wondering if you were going to come inside," she said.

"Yeah, I wasn't sure I was in the right place. Your street is so dark," I said, ascending the stairs two at a time.

"Oh I know! The electric company is rewiring the stop light up the road, and we haven't had streetlights for days now. It is kind of creepy." She rubbed her shoulders when I got to the top. I didn't quite know whether to hug her or just follow her into her apartment.

You could smell the food cooking from the hallway, and my mouth instantly watered. "How do these people live in the same building with you?" I said.

"Excuse me?" She was obviously confused by my statement.

"I don't think I could sit down the hall, smelling this mouthwatering food and not raid your apartment." We both laughed, but I was serious.

I followed her through the hallway, and the apartment building transformed into a luxury condo. Recess lighting and modern decor graced the entranceway. The kitchen was fit for a chef and was probably the big selling point for Claire. Granite countertops and a gas stove topped a large island in the kitchen and a smooth cream-colored set of cabinets lined the whole back wall. Her array of fresh fruits and vegetables were splayed out on the countertops beneath the cabinets and a spice rack that would make any chef proud took up one whole shelf in the pantry.

"This place is spectacular." I made a lap around the open concept living room, and I could see there was a loft bedroom up a narrow flight of stairs lining the back wall of the living room. "How long have you lived here?" I walked over to the large, floor to ceiling, windows, which were tinted to avoid anyone from seeing in. There were a set of automatic blinds that could be lowered at the push of a button. This place was the perfect bachelor pad or maybe couple's pad?

"Um, I have lived here for about six months now. I really love the layout of the apartment, and the people here keep to themselves." She was mixing something delectable in a bowl. I could smell a hint of seafood, and I could barely wait to taste whatever she was making.

"What's for dinner tonight?" I leaned over the counter towards her. She didn't seem nervous at all.

"Well, I have wanted to try this stuffed mushroom recipe . . ." she said as she slowly mixed whatever ingredients were stuffed into the powder blue mixing bowl.

"Yum!" I interjected bringing a smile to her face.

"And then there is this chocolate lava cake with a caramel sauce for dessert."

"Oh my God, Claire, stop." I laughed. "You had me at chocolate, anything after that is going to turn me into a drooling fool." I wasn't kidding. You ever hear that a way to a guy's heart is through his stomach? Well that is bullshit, but what is true is that if a girl can cook then she gets major points in the "could be my wife" category. So I can see the misconception, but there is a real difference.

Claire giggled but continued mixing her concoction. "So what all is in there?"

"Umm, it has some lump crab meat and mayonnaise with a whole bunch of spices. There is cilantro and Italian loaf bread crumbs. I am getting ready to add in a cup of grated cheddar cheese, and then I am going to stuff those portabella mushrooms and top them with more cheese." She listed off the ingredients like she was giving instructions to her staff.

"Sounds delicious! So what can I do?" I rubbed my hands together signaling that I didn't mind getting my hands dirty.

"Actually if you can just open this bottle of wine that would be super helpful."

I poured a few glasses and we toasted to a wonderful evening. I was a little bummed she didn't want my help in the kitchen. I hoped she wasn't one of those control freaks that wanted to conquer the world by themselves. Being independent and motivated was good, but not to the point where you shut your family out. I realized that was the definition of my father, which had been what sparked the resentment between us.

Claire and I talked seamlessly for another hour as she flitted around the kitchen pouring this and baking that. I felt like a lump on a log just waiting for her to get done. When dinner was finally ready, we sat down at her mahogany bar style table, and the night continued without a hitch.

The conversation between Claire and I flowed. Although I didn't feel any sparks, I thought we paired nicely. It's not that she wasn't beautiful because she was, but I felt like I was having dinner with an old friend instead of a new love. Dinner was spectacular. After, we sat down on the sofa, and she pulled her legs tightly up under her.

We talked for hours about food and movies. I learned a lot about her past dating history, and I selectively picked through the details of my life. I didn't want to risk being called a liar if I ever told her the truth.

"Wait a second," she said and popped off the couch.

"Okay?" I laughed.

Claire bounded into the kitchen almost spilling the wine sloshing around in her glass. She set down the glass and opened the fridge revealing a small plate with several square pieces of chocolate on it.

"Oh wow! What is that?" My mouth instantly watered, and she approached me with the sugary confections.

"These are my last surprise, if you can shove one more thing down your throat."

We both laughed, and I responded saying, "Are you kidding me? I can feel the pounds stacking up. I'm going to have to leave here and head straight to the gym."

"If you spend any more time at the gym, you won't be able to walk out in public without being mauled by a dozen women."

"So let me get this straight. Are you saying that I am borderline irresistible? Are you trying to hit on me? Because if you are, I'm flattered."

Blushing, she took a small piece of the chocolate and held it out. "Eat the chocolate, Drew." She didn't appear to be placing it in my hand, so I opened my mouth and she laid the chocolate on my tongue. She popped the other half in her own mouth and let it melt on her tongue.

"What do you taste?" she said. Her eyes lit with excitement.

"Hmmm!" I let the chocolate roll around in my mouth. I could taste some heat, but I couldn't quite place what flavor it was. "Is it some kind of chili flavor?" It was a wild guess, but I could definitely taste the spice. I sipped some wine to wash down the thick sludge leftover.

"Yeah, I have been playing with the flavors, and I think this is my favorite. What do you think?"

"I mean it's definitely different, but I am more of a sweet fan than savory. It's delicious though, just not my style." She had me try the others, which were pomegranate and strawberry. I preferred the strawberry. She said they were going to package the flavors to give as favors to the guests at her hotel.

"People would love that. It's very *unique*. I think you are on to something there. I would love to try a cinnamon version." The chocolate was out of this world, and the flavors were . . . different.

"Hmm! That is an idea." I could see the ideas checking off in her head as she sat down on the sofa next to me. "Do you have to work tomorrow?" That was the famous girl code for *get out*. So I took the bait.

"Yeah, actually I have to be up pretty early, but dinner was fantastic." I stood from the sofa towering above the petite chef. "Talk to you soon?" It was more of a question. I had waited patiently all night to see if she would show any signs of interest in me.

"Yeah, I'm going to be busy this week, but we'll have to get together again soon." She checked the clock hanging against the adjacent wall and gave a quick yawn. *Strike three, buddy, you're out.*

We parted ways, and I jogged through the dark empty street to my car. The drive home was full of thoughts, but they weren't about just Claire. Neither of us had attempted so much as a hug on the way out. It didn't feel necessary since I was leaving my "friend's" house. I thought back over Jenna and Sicily. I was beginning to wonder if any of the women I had contacted were my type. Then there was Beth. I had to find a way to see where that could go without my father hating me, but for now she was shelved. I couldn't risk ruining the work I had done over a girl that probably thought I was an idiot.

When I arrived home, I checked my inbox. I had my daily email from Victoria. We had been talking a lot, but she had never offered to give me her number or set up a real date. I liked talking to her though. She was down to earth and funny. I even liked hearing about her daughter who was in the first grade. Her name was Emmaline, and from what I had been told, she was incredibly smart and cute.

Victoria raved about her, which set off good signals for me. I wanted someone who had the capacity to care more about someone else than they did themselves. I didn't know if I was ready to be a role model for a six year old, but I did know I could support them. Was that enough though?

There was a second email from Lola. I hadn't heard from her since she sent me the flyer. The email said, "I'll be in the DJ booth until ten if you want to hang out. Just ask for Lola."

I knew that this would be an unforgettable evening, although I had serious doubts that she was the one for me. So far she had piqued my interest with her short messages and witty poems. She wasn't ugly by any means, but looking at her profile pictures gave me the feeling she might play with Ouija boards or practice witchcraft in her spare time.

Hey, maybe she'd cast a love spell on me? I replied letting her know I'd be there. Now I had to figure out what one wears to a rave.

I settled in to my bed that night and let my head sink in to the pillows, wishing for a better week; one free of criticism or letdowns. *Good luck with that.*

NINE

TUESDAY MORNING came quickly, but I was ready. I walked into the board meeting with my head held high. I had made several copies of my proposal to hand out during the board meeting. The board consisted of four people. Bob with benefits, my father, my mother, and Linda with accounting. The board members had been the original company before it got big. I had not expected, however, for Beth to join us that morning. She strode in wearing a gray dress suit with a white ruffled collar shirt and a pair of four-inch black stilettos. I couldn't recall the last time I saw her wear heels, but holy shit that is distracting.

The board was seated, and they discussed a few things regarding our numbers and the new clients. Then it was my turn. My mother winked as I stood up and adjusted my beige sports coat. I didn't chance a look at Beth, but I could tell out of the corner of my eye that she was chewing on her pen. I handed out the copies of my report and started my speech. I said blah blah blah about the employees needing to feel comfortable and appreciated at work. I laid out the whole plan to make the changes and then we got down to the numbers.

My father sat arms crossed and face void of any emotion. My mother looked like she would burst into tears of joy and pride at any moment. The other two seemed impressed while Beth appeared to be off in her own little world.

I finished the list and then stood there waiting for the applause; it didn't happen. I did get a semi positive response though.

"Well, son, I see you took this very seriously, and I think we can agree these changes are necessary to stay relevant. We will vote on the changes and let you know. You are excused now."

I wanted to protest. I didn't know why I couldn't be present for the vote. It wasn't as if I had a personal interest in the changes. Beth followed me out so the board could conclude their meeting.

I headed back to my office feeling more than a little irritated.

"Hey Drew, will you slow down?" I turned to see Beth briskly walking down the hallway towards me. I stopped to allow her to catch up and then continued to my office.

"What is it, Beth?" I didn't mean for it to sound so rude, but the way I was dismissed to allow the *grownups* to talk was belittling.

She didn't say anything until we were safely behind my closed office door. "They liked your proposal. I could tell by your dad's face, so why did you storm out of there like a five year old?" She sat down in one of the comfy leather chairs across from me and crossed her arms and legs simultaneously. Watching those smooth legs slide over each other and those *do me* heels dangling on her feet was sexy enough without even rising high enough to see her face. I had noticed at my parents' house she wore contacts, but at work she had black rimmed square glasses. Staring at her face, I wasn't sure which I preferred.

"It's just that my father is so arrogant when he speaks to me. He acts like I am not capable of completing one correct task. Like I'm a child." I flicked my wrist in the air as I spouted off all the things that pissed me off about my father. Beth just listened.

When I was finished, she licked her lips and uncrossed her legs. She leaned forward with her elbows on my desk and said, "Drew, you have to give him a chance. You haven't exactly been employee of the month since you started here, and your father doesn't know how to address that." She put her hand on top of mine and said, "Just give him a chance."

Her hand lingered on mine until my office door opened, and she jerked her head around. My mother's head poked in and the smile on her face always made me calm down.

"You did great, honey. We all agreed to your plan. Your father even said it was well written, and he would like to speak with you, with you both actually, after lunch today." She paused and waited for our response. We nodded and she shut the door behind her, repeating her praise of my project.

Beth's eyes looked like saucers when she turned around. I was happy to see that even she felt intimidated by my father, and he actually liked her. Beth left for lunch, and I snacked on a pack of crackers while I checked my email. I had a few responses today. Victoria messaged that her daughter would be gone tomorrow evening at a Vacation Bible School with her church, and she would have an hour or so available if I wanted to meet. I emailed her my cell number and asked that she let me know the time and the place.

Lola sent me another poem about rocking out to the beat and moving my feet. The corny lines made me smile, and I could tell that she was being silly. I needed silly. Carefree fun without all the drama.

Two o'clock rolled around, and I was chewing the nubs on my fingers. I wasn't looking forward to this meeting with my dad. And to be honest, being around Beth was becoming taxing.

I walked down the hallway to my father's office, but as I approached the glass double doors, I could see that Beth was already in there. My father was laughing heartily, and Beth looked relaxed and comfortable in the chair across for him. My hopes perked up that they didn't have the same feeling of doom. I walked through the door, and the laughter immediately stopped. I swear I felt all the air sucked out of the room, leaving me breathless with a softball-sized lump in my throat.

"Am I late?" I said with a smile. I tried to push through my racing thoughts to focus on their reaction. Beth didn't even turn to look at me while my father's face twisted to face me.

"No, son, we were just talking about you. I was telling Beth that I was pleased with your proposal." He clasped his hands on the desk, and I could feel a "but" coming on. "I am sure you are aware of the Aviation Conference coming up this weekend. Your mother is nagging me about some cruise I supposedly agreed to and it leaves on Thursday." He waved his hands around showing his frustration while I slid my hands in my pockets and waited for the other shoe to drop. "So son, what I am asking is whether you would mind stepping in for me? Beth will be there to guide you. She has been there a few times already, and she knows the drill."

I could see Beth smooth her skirt out of the corner of my eye. "Uh yeah, that sounds great. What do I need to do?"

"Well for starters, the conference is in Atlanta, and I have scheduled a flight for the two of you at nine Friday morning. Also we have commissioned a booth to display our services and give information to the agents. The plane you are taking is the new plane, and it will be on display for tours after the conference." My father continued explaining our detailed instructions. I looked at Beth who seemed to tense up when our eyes met.

"Beth, have I forgotten anything?" She practically jumped at the mention of her name.

"No, Mr. Sloane, I think you have covered it all." She rose from her chair and rushed past me out of the door. When the door shut behind her, my father turned to me and the smile drained from his face.

"Son, I don't have to tell you again how important it is not to mix business with pleasure." His accusing tone almost triggered an eye roll, but I managed to stand there and listen to his lecture while simultaneously removing Beth's skirt in my mind. I snapped back into reality just in time for my father to dismiss me. His parting words were that Beth would be in touch with me about the set up for the booth. I walked back towards my desk, passing Beth's empty cubicle on my way. I decided to swing by the lounge to see if my new "partner" was grabbing a drink. Sure enough, there she was, bent over in the fridge, reaching for something in the bottom drawer. Her tight skirt clung to her legs, and she struggled to bend far enough to reach her snack.

"So my father said you needed to talk with me?" I said loud enough to get her attention. She rose quickly, bumping her head on the roof of the refrigerator. I rushed forward to help her, but she quickly straightened and huffed out her frustration. She took a moment to steady herself and I, being the good guy, grabbed a bag labeled with her name out of the drawer.

"Yes," she huffed. "Apparently it's you and me this weekend, and I need to walk through the layout with you. Your father has preapproved the exhibit, but it is likely you will be questioned, and I need you to know how to answer."

"Understood. So when do we start?" The weekend was only a few days away, and I was anxious to get started, with her.

"I have asked for the board room tomorrow so we can practice the exhibit there, and the plane is being fueled and cleaned for this weekend, so we will tour that on Thursday."

The thought sprang into my head that the rave was Thursday. It shouldn't be a problem for me to be at the airport at nine. I would need to pack ahead of course, but it wouldn't be the first all-nighter I had pulled.

Beth snapped her fingers, and I glanced her way. "Drew! Did I lose you somewhere?" She placed one petite hand on her not so petite hip and stared at me through her deep blue eyes.

"No, I was just thinking about what I should wear."

"A suit, Drew. You have to take this seriously." She turned to leave snatching away her mysterious snack bag, and I reached for her arm.

"I am trying here, Beth. I have been to work on time. I am taking my assignments seriously. What do I have to do to prove myself?"

Beth looked shocked for a moment right before her face twisted into a frown. "I don't know, Drew, but let's start with this conference."

"I won't let you down." She nodded and headed back to her desk with her snack. I was looking forward to this trip and a little alone time with Beth. I just needed to stay focused.

TEN

WHEN I GOT HOME that evening, my message box was flashing on my computer. "Hey Drew, I was hoping you could meet me at the Hope Park on Fifth Street tomorrow at six forty-five. I am dropping Emma off at six thirty. Maybe we could have dinner at the park? My treat!——Victoria"

The single mom thing was growing on me. I had this crazy idea that I could somehow fit into their family. They needed a man to help support them, and I was in a position to do that. So far Victoria hadn't made me feel uncomfortable or inadequate. She hadn't put any pressure on me to be something that I wasn't. I wanted someone like that to accept me as I am with no judgment. Beth had obviously judged me pretty harshly, and I wasn't exactly sure how I felt about that. I mean, she didn't even know me. I didn't know whether to view her as a challenge or a caution sign. I emailed Victoria back and headed to the kitchen for dinner. Thankfully my father wasn't home, and I could relax at the table with my mom.

We had a steady flow of conversation where she asked me about my personal life, and I gave her a few tidbits about me dating. I couldn't believe that out of all the girls, so far none had worked out. Maybe I'm too picky or maybe I was destined to be with someone who only tolerated me for my money.

That was a hugely depressing thought.

"Mom, what was it about Dad that made you realize he was the one?"

"Your father is a wonderful man, and from the time I laid eyes on him I knew that I just had to have him. He's funny and outgoing and kind. He always made me laugh and feel *special.*"

"You mean he *was* all of those things. Now all I see is an arrogant . . ."

"Andrew!" His mother hissed. "Now I know that your father can be . . . difficult, but he loves you more than anything."

I dropped my spoon, and it clanged against the side of the plate. "I don't know how you can allow him to treat you with such disrespect. He is barely around, and he leaves you by yourself all the time. You are a wonderful person, and he doesn't even see it."

"Yes, he does. That is the beauty about finding someone that knows you better than you know yourself. You begin to realize that sometimes it is more important to support someone else's dreams and set aside your own. This is his dream and who am I to take it away?"

I couldn't believe the load of bull that she believed. They could both have their dreams without him casting her aside. I went upstairs to pick out my clothes for the next day. I planned to leave straight from the office to meet Victoria. She was only a few miles north of the runway.

I heard the buzz sounding from the gate, and I wondered who would drop by on a Tuesday night. I pressed the button and said, "Come on up!" It didn't occur to me until after that it might be a murderer, and I just buzzed them through. When I opened the door, I realized that I would have preferred the murderer.

"Camille!" I said sounding just as shocked as I was feeling. "What are you doing here?" She had eyeliner running down her cheek.

"Can we talk?" She shifted in her too high heels and a small part of me felt sorry for her. Sorry enough to let her in? Ehhh.

"Yeah, come on in." I ushered her up to my room, and she plunked down on the leather sofa across from the bed. I sat on the edge of the bed and prepared myself for the sob story coming next. "What's going on? You don't look like yourself!" *Good, Drew, real good. Just insult her in her already fragile state.*

She dropped her hands down and said, "Thanks! You're a real gentleman, ya know?" She twisted in her seat, and I could see the smooth layer of skin rising all the way up to the crease in between. I made the mistake of raising my eyebrows, which she immediately caught on to.

She rose off the couch and started towards me. I was prepared to listen to her story, not fight off this gorgeous woman who was giving me the sultry looks that I knew all too well. *Stop her, Drew! Say no right now and tell her goodnight!* I pleaded with myself.

"Camille!" I said holding up my hands when she reached me. She ran her long smooth fingers along the lines of my neck. *Too late!* I hadn't been with anyone since Camille, and we broke up weeks ago. I didn't want her to get the wrong idea, but I could definitely use the release.

"What, Drew? You don't want me?" From my spot on the bed, I was eye level with her supple breasts. Another few inches and I would be buried in between them. Not a bad place to be.

I put my hands on her hips and resisted the urge to squeeze the flesh beneath them. Camille was a beautiful woman.

"Camille, why are you here?" I had to close my eyes when I pushed her away extending her back as far as my arms could reach. I looked directly at her eyes and said, "I am with someone else now."

"Who?" she screeched.

I had to stop myself from smiling when I thought about the answer to that question. Claire, Victoria, Lola . . . take your pick. "That's not the point, Camille."

She stepped forward and placed her legs on either side of my mine and pushed me back on the bed. "Well whoever she is . . ." she said, running her hand down my chest. "She isn't me!"

She leaned down and licked the spot under my ear. She knew that made me crazy. She knew exactly what I liked and how to break through my puny defenses. Isn't that what I needed? Someone who knew how to please me? I mean I wasn't exclusive with any of the girls I was dating.

"Camille, you know we aren't getting back together, right? It's just not going to work." I waited for her to rise up; to get up and leave the house in a huff, but she didn't.

Instead she kept going, licking the base of my neck. I wanted to resist, but who could resist someone so beautiful. "Camille!" I said and put my hands on her shoulders.

"Drew, I get it. We aren't going to be together, but right now, I need this. I need someone to make me feel good. I need you just like this and then I'll leave. No strings." She held up her hand as if to say "Scout's honor."

I nodded and she continued the assault on my neck. I relaxed and let her take my shirt off. I watched as she stood and shimmied off the sparkly halter-top she was wearing and slid the lacy thong down her long, tan legs. I slid higher on the bed and relaxed on the plush pillows at the top. She didn't remove her bra, which was black and lacy like her panties. She kept on the black wavy skirt as well; I almost preferred the slightly covered look. I liked the way my hands slid in between the smooth material and the silky skin beneath.

She reached into my nightstand and grabbed the foil packet sealing the deal between us. She climbed back on top of me and unbuttoned my pants; she slid them down and then ran her finger beneath my boxers. My whole body tensed as she pulled them down and mounted me.

"Damn, Camille!" She was a pro when it came to pleasure, something that I had conveniently forgotten when I dumped her.

She was quick to release which didn't help my growing need to explode inside her. I let her do all the work at first. She grinded and rolled her hips against me. I ran my hands across the smooth flesh on her stomach.

I knew I was getting close, and I ached to have more control over the moments. I pulled her to me and rolled us over. She looked beautiful beneath me with her hair splayed out on the pillows. She had a devious smile on her face like she had won somehow. I thrust forward a few more times, and she arched her back in the air. The friction between us sent me over the edge. It felt amazing to release the pent up frustration and uncertainty. I collapsed on the bed beside her, and she rolled towards me putting her head on my shoulder.

It felt good, but I knew I couldn't let this happen. As great as it felt to be inside her, I knew that being with her was settling for someone who couldn't be what I needed. I instantly regretted letting her in. I gave her a few more minutes before I got up to get dressed. I didn't want to be like wham bam thank you ma'am, so I put some pants on and sat on the couch.

"Where are you going?" She pulled the ruffled covers up and rolled over on her side to face me. Her lacy bra could barely hold in her engorged breasts. You could barely tell they were bought and paid for.

"Now do you want to tell me why you are here?" I reached into the mini fridge and pulled out a beer. I offered one to her, but she declined.

"I miss you, Drew. I have dated a lot of guys and none of them make me feel like you do. I want us to get back together." She slung her legs over the bed and came to sit with me on the couch.

"Camille, I told you that I am dating someone now, and I really like her. I don't think we are a match. I want something besides the partying and the trips." I felt like such an ass as the words poured out. I should have never let her in.

A single tear fell down her face. "I thought I could count on you to help me."

"Help you with what?"

She crossed her arms and perched her bare feet on the glass coffee table. "Ricardo kicked me out, and I don't have a place to stay. I thought I could crash here for a few days." I hated seeing her upset even though I wasn't willing to let her back into my life.

I grabbed my wallet and pulled out a few large bills. "Here," I said. "This should hold you over for a few days until you figure it out." It wasn't what she wanted, but there was no way we could live together here, especially with me going out of town in a few days. It had to be enough.

She had no qualms with taking the money. She took the money and crunched it up in her hand. "Yeah, thanks." She smeared a few more tears off her cheek and leaned in for a hug. "It's not what I wanted, but it'll have to work, I guess."

"You can't stay with your parents?" I knew for a fact that her parents were willing to let her stay *if* she was willing to go by their rules. They were tired of her partying and the guys she dated.

"Yeah, if I want to be a prisoner," she snarked.

"Might not be a bad thing to take a step back and figure out what's important to you. That's what I am trying to do."

"You are a good guy, Drew. I wish I could be more like you . . . focused and practical. You know I used to want to be a nurse. I wanted to help people and somehow that all got mixed up."

"It's not too late, Camille; you can go back to school. I'd help you, and your parents would help. Just think about it."

She hugged me tight and ruffled her hands through my hair. I kissed her forehead. My lips lingered a bit longer on her forehead than I felt comfortable with, but she was obviously in need of some reassurance. When I walked her out the front door, she seemed a little more hopeful. I wanted her to be happy, and I meant what I said about helping her, but I didn't love her. I leaned into her car, and she kissed my cheek. I watched her car leave and headed back to the porch just in time to see my parents pull into the drive. My parents were less than impressed with Camille or her behavior. The look I got from them made me feel instantly ashamed. What a night this had turned out to be.

ELEVEN

BETH HAD SPENT the entire day grilling me on the set up. She had not even allowed me to help create the presentation. She hadn't been unpleasant really, but she had treated me like a child. She even went as far as to create a set of note cards to help me with my lines.

Whatever.

I was content to sit quietly, only responding when she asked me to or mindlessly nodding that I understood. We took a break for lunch where I retreated to my office to check my email.

"Hey, Drew. I can't wait to meet you this afternoon. I'll be waiting at the bench next to the volleyball net. -Victoria!"

Her excitement was contagious. I was very excited to meet her as well. I did harbor a bit of guilt about my interaction with Camille the night before, but I was banking on the fact that I wasn't exclusive with any of them yet.

I was also excited about the rave the next night. Not so excited about my early morning flight. Or the flight itself for that matter. I hated flying.

I hated the takeoff, the landing, watching the clouds zoom by, etc.

On the other hand, of course there was Beth. We would be on our trip for three days, and that was totally worth the near death experience. I hoped.

At quitting time, I headed to the bathroom down the hall and checked my appearance. I had worn a pair of jeans and a button up collared shirt. I'd chosen it because the blues and grays in the shirt brought out the color of my eyes. *I was turning into such a girl.*

"Alrighty then, so I guess we have about covered the presentation, and I'll see you tomorrow for the plane walk through so you can get familiar with the layout and all of the features. Do you have any questions?" Her eyes blinked quickly as she waited for my response.

"No, I think I got it." Trying to save what little dignity I had after her grade school teaching lesson, I turned and retreated out of the conference room and back into the kitchen to check out the newly installed vending machines. They were incredible if I do say so myself. It included a beverage machine, which housed sodas and juices and a pair of hot and cold snack machines, which included muffins, sandwiches, and an array of candy and chips. I was in heaven checking out the shiny pack of peanut M&Ms. I swiped my card and watched the bright yellow bag drop into the bin. I snatched it up and ripped the plastic spilling the chocolate into my palm.

"I see you found the machines." Beth pulled her hands behind her back, and I nodded trying not to throw some smartass comment in her direction. "They are great. You made a good choice in selecting them."

"Thanks!" I mumbled through the mouthful of chocolate. I knew it was impolite, but after that morning's ABC lesson I was interested in being *charming.*

"Okay." She shrugged. Looking as if she was holding back, I continued to stare waiting for her to finish what she need to say, but she was silent until she spun around on her heels and exited the room.

Weird, right? What was she trying to accomplish? Did she want me to thank her for treating me like a child? She insulted me one minute and praised me the other. Brushing off that strange experience, I headed back to my office to get my things.

When I arrived at the park, my engine seemed to startle the park's quiet setting. I got out of the car and strolled slowly to the bench. When I got closer, I could see the long flowing strawberry blonde hair from behind. I could tell she needed a root touch up and that she was wearing a pink spaghetti strap dress with a see through white knit shawl. She seemed classy in her own right. I introduced myself and the smile that spread across her face was enough to make me feel instantly comfortable.

"Oh my goodness, it's nice to finally meet you!" She stood and hugged me, lightly patting my back, which reminded me of my mom. Maybe it was a mom thing? I invited her to walk the jogging trail with me. She wrapped her arm around mine, and we slowly walked around the track talking about everything from the weather to work. She was bubbly and sweet.

We stopped at the concession truck, and she got a strawberry ice cream in a waffle cone, while I got a plain vanilla in a sugar cone. Sitting at a bench eating ice cream, we continued to admire the beauty of the park.

"I've never actually been here before," I admitted.

"Really? I bring Emmaline here almost every sunny day. She loves playing on the swings over there." She pointed to the wooden swing set next to the jungle gym. "We adopted a puppy from the pound last weekend." Her eyes lit up with excitement as she explained, "He's a mutt, so we aren't sure which breed he is, but he is brown with black feet. Em named him Tyson, like the boxer."

"Oh that's cute," I said. "I've never had a puppy. My parents were never the type to take on living animals except for me of course, but I'm an only child so . . ."

"That's horrible. You couldn't have been that bad as a child." She seemed so interested in what I was saying that I wanted to keep talking.

"Maybe. No, I was perfect." Victoria's laughter far exceeded my own, but I was content to watch her head fly back and her mouth open wide as she giggled over my confession.

Around the time the sun slowly creeped down over the hills, Victoria looked at her watch and visibly frowned.

"I guess it's time for me to get going," she said.

We stood on the path hand in hand as we said goodbye. I could honestly say that I had enjoyed the walk. I didn't quite know about sparks yet, but I liked her.

She lifted up on her tippy toes and planted a kiss on my cheek. She smoothed away the remaining lipstick with the pad of her thumb. "All right, Drew, I had a wonderful time. I hope to hear from you soon."

I waved goodbye as she crossed the parking lot. The evening was so nice I decided to make another lap around the track. This time I focused on the scenery instead of the beautiful girl that was standing next to me. Even the kid thing didn't have me scared anymore. Victoria seemed like a great mom. I wondered how she'd be as a lover. She had mentioned that her child's father had skipped out early on. She got pregnant when she was seventeen, and the father wasn't keen on losing his party years to a crying infant. I admired her for doing it on her own and being self-sufficient with hopes and goals.

I hadn't told her much about me, other than my three-date rule. She said she would look forward to planning that second date if I was interested. I told her it would be my pleasure to see her again and I had meant it. I was curious to see what she would pick. I was not looking forward to another cram session at work the next day. I could only imagine what Beth had planned for me to "learn."

We were supposed to tour the private jet, and I had to start packing for the three-day conference. I knew Thursday night would likely be a blur, and we were heading out early Friday morning.

To my surprise, and I was feeling surprised a lot lately, Beth did not come in to work on Thursday. She had still managed to leave an impossible schedule for me. She had been on the plane several times so she missed the tour, but she was kind enough to place sticky notes everywhere.

"Fully stocked mini fridge." Uh duh! What kind of party boy would I be if I didn't know what that was? "King sized bedroom!" There was only one bedroom on this plane, but the luxury plane only carried up to six passengers at a time, if that many. The layout of the plane was quite impressive. The amenities could include a four star chef, a masseuse, a hair and makeup stylist, and even a personal tour guide for the destination you were traveling to; for the right price, of course.

I left a tad bit early from work on Thursday. I cleared it, of course. I really did need to finish packing, and well, I wanted to take a nap before I hit the rave to meet Lola. I packed my suitcase in record time, not overlooking any of my toiletries and "hang out" clothes. I hoped to do a lot of hanging out by the pool at the hotel. I wished we were headed somewhere more tropical, but Georgia was nice this time of year. I did a few searches to get used to the neighborhood. There was a farmers' market and a lot of cool shops down the street from the hotel. There were also a string of bars and one very interesting dance club a few miles away. I wondered how Beth would feel about joining me for drinks and maybe a dance. Honestly she seemed a little uptight about "out of work" functions and there was no telling what my father had told her about me.

She probably thought I came equipped with an entourage of not-so-uptight girls. I planned to show her a different side of me.

I laid down for a nap that wasn't going to happen, but it did give me some quiet time for reflection on the last few weeks. It was weird how it all was working out. I was still getting emails from new people. Most of them weren't my type at all, but there were a few that I liked. It was strange how comfortable I had become with these meet and greets. I enjoyed getting to know the new girls. The thought alone of Victoria made me smile. And while Claire and a few of the others hadn't worked out, the dates had been fun and eye-opening. Each one, good or bad, had been a clue to whom I would ultimately want.

Camille had been on my mind a lot today. I don't know if it was guilt or worry, but I knew I hadn't heard the last from her. She would be back to ask for money or look for some sort of comfort. I hoped that she would take my advice about moving home and getting her life together. I closed my eyes and watched the highlight reel. The girl's smiles and giggles were flashing by, as well as, my checklist of likes/dislikes.

Wants a family/good mother—Victoria

Knows the difference between wealth and happiness—Claire

Good values/work ethic—Beth

Funny and good sense of humor—Lola

It was so hard to decipher what I wanted in a woman, but I was slowly figuring it out. I opened my eyes to check the clock. Two hours had gone by. I must have fallen asleep at some point. I hopped up to get ready. The club was forty-five minutes away, and I had decided to take my suitcases with me to avoid the drive back time. I could just as easily board the plane and sleep there until it was time to go.

I hopped in my car and revved up the motor. When the garage door opened, I almost had a heart attack. Standing with arms crossed in front of the car was my father. I put the car back in park and got out of the car. He didn't look happy, and I had about three guesses why.

"Hey, what's up?" I said. He didn't smile or move for that matter. I hated how he tried to stare me down or intimidate me into doing what he wanted. I tried my best not to be disrespectful, but it didn't come out that way. "Look, Father, I am not a mind reader, so you can stare all you want, but if you aren't planning to tell me what's wrong I can't fix it."

"What's up?" he said holding his hands up in the air like a crazy person. "Is that you have a very important weekend ahead of you and here you are heading out after dark in a Grateful Dead T-shirt like you are heading to a party. Son, if you really want to be a part of this company then I need you to put your job first and your social life second." His arms resumed their crossed position. I was speechless. *Well, maybe not speechless!*

"Father, when are you going to realize that I am a capable adult; capable of balancing work and fun? I have worked my butt off in the last few weeks on the mindless projects you have given me, and I am more than prepared to handle this weekend. But that does not mean that I am not allowed time to do what I want when I am off the clock. My bags are packed, and I am ready to go."

I got back in the car, and he stormed out of the garage back to the main house. I revved the engine so loud that when I pressed the gas pedal it spun out of the driveway. I was more determined than ever to have a good time tonight and to rock this trip over the weekend.

I arrived at the club a little after nine thirty. The oversized steel building was completely lit up by lime green and blue strobe lights and spotlights hitting every angle. I had worn as much black as my closet would allow so that I would fit in better.

When I entered the club I was instantly impressed. It was like a mixture of half nude, half gothic patrons. Girls wore mini plaid skirts that didn't even cover their panties while most of the guys were shirtless with the most insane tattoos and piercings. People on swings and in cages danced and convulsed to the rhythm. If it wasn't for the fun atmosphere and the deafening music, I might have been scared.

I was still reeling from the fight between my dad and me, so I headed straight to the bar. They didn't serve beer, so the bartender passed me a menu with some drink names I had never heard. I felt like a freak asking for a Misty Unicorn—a mixture of Vodka, Sprite and a shot of Red Bull.

Once I had my drink, I made my way down the bar and to the DJ booth. I hung around a table near the front and took in the sights. People were grinding and biting each other while others did body shots off the model worthy girls lying on the tables. People donned every color of the rainbow in glow lights.

A voice came over the microphone. It was a female's voice, and although I couldn't see into the booth, I imagined it was Lola.

"Hey ladies! Look to the sky as the heavens open up and the sky is raining men."

It's Raining Men came on briefly to introduce the guys, but then it faded into a faster beat. I wasn't ready for the ribbons to drop down from the ceiling and a bunch of men wearing some underwear meant for ladies, in my opinion, came sliding down the ribbon. The women in the audience went crazy and money was flying everywhere. The guys twirled and descended the ribbons repeatedly until the song was over. Then they climbed back up to the rafters and disappeared into the darkness. I was impressed; it was creepy but definitely impressive.

TWELVE

I CHECKED MY WATCH at ten o'clock exactly and downed the rest of my drink. I made my way to the DJ booth, which created its own set of problems. I could feel people grabbing and grinding against me. I was pretty sure I got licked along the way somewhere.

I approached a very large man who automatically put his hand up to stop me. "Hey, I am here to see Lola."

"And who are you?" he barked. I wasn't nearly drunk enough to take on this tank of a person. I opened my mouth to speak, but then a bleach blonde head popped around the corner.

"It's okay, Jax. I told him he could come up."

She disappeared around the corner, and I pointed in her direction. "Yeah, what she said." He only grunted in response and opened the chain gate to let me by. I climbed the narrow set of stairs into the DJ booth. The alcohol from the drink had me feeling buzzed, and when I combined that with the rush of meeting Lola and the pumped up music, I was ready to dance.

"Hey there, I'm Drew." I reached my hand out and she held up a finger in my face. She put her headphones on and pressed a red button on her board.

"All right guys, it's your turn to scream. Ladies . . . show them how it's done!" Screams erupted from everywhere and swings came down from the ceiling at warp speed. Girls in lingerie riding swings, dangled from the rafters. They leaned all the way back with only their feet hanging on to the ropes. They stood on the swings and danced to the beat of *Talk Dirty to Me*.

It was sultry and seductive, and I was really warming up to the idea of hanging out at this club. I turned my attention back to Miss Lola. She was wearing a black mini skirt with mismatched zippers strategically spaced out. Her shirt was a white and black plaid corset. Her bleach blonde hair was twirled in black tinged pigtails. Her black boots laced all the way up to her thighs. She was freaking hot. She was different, but incredibly sexy in her own way.

Lola removed her headphones and her bubbly excitement spilled over. "Hi there, cutie! I wasn't sure if you were going to make it." She wrapped her arms around me in a quick hug. She smelled like cotton candy that I assumed was the flavor of her bright blue lip-gloss smeared across her lips. The chill from the metal chain hanging around her neck seared into my arm.

"Yeah, this place is awesome!" I took a step back and gave her a once over look. "And you look amazing!" She winked and did like a half curtsy. "Can I get you a drink?"

"I have a break in a few, and we can go down together. I am anxious to see how you look on the dance floor." She was cool and confident; traits I was very much interested in meeting. Jax reached around the corner and shouted out a song request. She held one long polished finger up and I nodded, giving her space. She played the shout out and, then a man with a giant nose ring and a scull tattooed on his *actual* skull came to relieve her. I couldn't help but lift my eyebrows at the replacement.

Whoa!

I followed her like a lovesick puppy to the bar. Her cute frilly skirt swayed with each step as she sauntered to the bar and ordered herself a vampire cocktail. I asked for the same, although I had my doubts about what the cocktail might taste like.

When they slid the yellow drink across the table with a syringe full of some sort of red goo, I reminded myself that I *was* going to have a good time tonight despite my father's warning.

"To a good night with hot people!" she screamed above the music. We held our glasses up and clinked them together. I could barely hear her words above the music so I still had no idea how to drink this. I watched as she removed her syringe from her glass and motioned for me to do the same. Together, we downed the orange flavored drink shot, and I let the vodka burn its way down my throat, further igniting the fire in my chest. I was well on my way to being wasted. Then she took my syringe and asked me to open my mouth. I was hesitant to say the least. I twisted my lips sideways showing my hesitation.

"Come on, it's good!" She laughed. She threw back her head, and then held her syringe up in the air and let the gooey liquid seep down her throat. I couldn't imagine anything looking sexier than she did right there swallowing down the red concoction. She swished the sauce in her mouth and gulped it down. She held my syringe back up, and I opened my mouth. It tasted like a sludgy raspberry Jell-O shot and it was a perfect end to the tangy orange flavored cocktail.

"That's good, right?" She nodded her head obviously able to tell that I was enjoying the drink.

"Actually yeah, that is really good!"

She slid our glasses across the bar and dragged me to the dance floor. "I love this song!" she said dancing and spinning around. I tried to keep up, but it really wasn't my style. I tried mimicking the guys near me, but they were out there. They reminded me of the break-dancers on TV, and I wasn't anywhere near that flexible or coordinated.

Lola was dancing circles around me. I pulled her close where she continued dancing and spinning. She put her hands on my shoulders and pulled my face closer, and I rested my forehead on hers. I enjoyed the way she rubbed up against me and kept a constant connection with my eyes. I hadn't noticed until now how incredibly dark gray her eyes were. You could almost see the stars in them the way they danced in the spotlight. I wondered briefly if they were contacts.

I could feel the sweat beading up on my forehead. It was so hot in the warehouse, and all the bodies crowded against me were suffocating. Although the music was growing on me, the electric beats and the rhythmic lights made me feel more buzzed than I should be after two drinks. I made another trip to the bar for Lola. She had insisted I get us the "Black Widow." When the bar tended gave me the drink, I could tell that it was another vodka-based cocktail. The mostly clear drink had a mystifying dark purple smear spreading through it. I waited until I got back to Lola to drink mine, and once again we toasted, this time to "meeting new people."

I liked her . . . a lot. She was so relaxed in our conversation. I couldn't imagine her meeting my parents, but they would have to get used to whomever I picked. After we downed the grape infused cocktail, she dragged me to a corner of the room. This section was gated with a line extended half way around the room, but Lola strode right past the line and simply patted the bouncer on the shoulder who immediately let us through.

We ended up in a quiet, secluded room. I could barely hear the pounding music in the pumping through the warehouse, but what I could hear was the sound her voice when she was whispering in my ear. It was hot! She was hot. She had a hint of sassiness in her voice, which grew a bit demanding as she ordered me to shut the curtains behind me.

I briefly wondered how many people she might have met in this room before now or what would happen if some brave soul brought a black light in there. I couldn't figure out whether she had any intention of starting a relationship with me or if she was only looking for a good time. Briefly I wondered and then I realized that I didn't give a damn what she had planned. I was borderline drunk and on my way to what was about to be the best make-out session I had ever had.

Lola smashed her lips against mine for one earth shattering second. When she pulled back, I questioned whether she even meant to do it. The stunned look on her face and the way she brought her fingers to her lips made me question if that giant spark was going to be lighting any fires.

"Wow!" I said. She smiled from behind her hand.

"So how do you like your first rave?" She recovered quickly. Her pale cheeks were flushed, and she was chewing on the end of her long spider web patterned nails.

"It's awesome! This place is great, and I'm getting used to the noise level. It makes you feel like you are on fire." I leaned back on the painted black doorframe staring at the glow in the dark star stickers stuck to the roof and let the buzzing sensations in my head build up. Lola looked as if she was torn and then all of a sudden she was on me, well, I was on her. She pulled me down by my shoulders onto the red leather sofa/bench thing. I had one hand on the back of the bench and one on the metal table bolted to the floor.

She tasted like the sweet drinks we had been downing, and I finally got a taste of those plump cotton candy lips. Her lips twisted around mine. She wrapped her nails around my shoulders and squeezed down. I had never been a fan of torture, but with her, the pain felt like an accelerator to the fire ripping through me. Pulling me closer by my hair, she positioned my head next to her neck. I smelled her first; I inhaled her sweet scent and then reached in to nibble on the silky white flesh.

She smashed my face into her neck, pulling me tighter and directing me to the spots she wanted me to kiss. I ran my hand up her thigh and around the hem of her skirt. Her skin felt so smooth underneath the rough fabric. I tried out the whole biting craze, sinking my teeth in little by little. I had to pull away because it felt so good I worried it might hurt her. When I pulled back, she looked directly in my eyes and screeched, "Don't stop!"

Diving back in, I made a trail of kisses from her collarbone down to her breasts, which were spilling out of the corset top. Holy shit, she was hot.

She wrapped one leg around my hip and lifted herself to me. I slid my arm underneath her back and closed the gap between us.

In the state I was in, I was completely ready to untie the constricting clothing she was wearing and let her take me to a place I hadn't gone before.

"Lola! You in here?" A deep voice shouted through the hallways. I could hear footsteps walking back to where we were. I pulled her up to a sitting position as the footsteps got closer. I could hear squeals from the adjacent rooms as the bouncer checked room to room for the missing DJ. We both looked dazed and confused when the bouncer rounded the corner.

The giant bouncer, Jax, was barreling towards the room saying, "Hey Lola, you're up." She nodded and he left as quickly as he entered, and I let out the breath I had been holding.

Lola burst out laughing, and I joined her. She grabbed my hand, and I pulled her to me. She landed one more mind-blowing kiss on me before she walked away. I sat there on the sofa for a moment trying to push back the overwhelming need that threatened to escape.

I walked back out to the dance floor and over to the DJ booth. Jax let me up with a smile this time, and I worried about whether I had lipstick somewhere. My hair was all over the place, and I shuttered thinking about how she pushed her fingers in my hair scratching her way through.

When I got up the narrow stairs, I saw Lola waiting at the top. She was sitting with her legs spread on the stool and, she was staring straight into my eyes with a sexy come-hither look. I walked briskly to her and slid in between those milky white thighs. People were still going bananas on the dance floor below, but I only had eyes for her.

"Damn, Lola! You are making me crazy." I was trying to catch my breath, but she just kept pulling me in deeper.

The song ended and she threw her hand back to start another. "Drew, right?" The fact that she wasn't sure what my name was, definitely set off red flags, but I nodded anyway. Maybe it was the kiss that wiped her memory. "You are an amazing kisser, Drew. I'd love to do this all night, but I have to get back to it."

Stunned. Confused. What was the word I was looking for? *Hmmm. Ah, yes! Blue balls.* Isn't that what you get when a woman drops you cold turkey after getting you all worked up. *Thanks a lot.*

"Yeah, me too. Work, I mean. I have an early flight to catch, but I'd like to see you again." *Yeah, I'd like to see you back in that room in about five minutes.* I tried to act cool like what she was doing wasn't completely blowing my mind. Was she trying to play hard to get?

"Oh cool, well enjoy your trip." She turned back to her table, dismissing my question to meet again. I walked up behind her and rubbed my hands down her arms. She had to be as torn up as I was. "Drew, I'll text you or something, okay?"

Just like that, the trance was broken. I stood there like a chump.

I thought about confronting her and pleading my case. I wanted to tell her how much I liked her poems and how much fun I was having, but pride and confusion held me in my place. I turned around on my heel, possibly a bit too fast as the thoughts in my head were spinning at warp speed. Heading out of the booth, I paid my tab at the counter and made my way to the door. What was her deal? I mean, she kissed me and I knew she liked it, so why the ice cold act?

I checked my watch on my way out, and it was one-thirty; not too bad. I hopped in my car and drove straight to the airport. Any remnants of a buzz had been stripped away by Lola in there so I felt comfortable driving. Hell, the confusion was more of a distraction as I replayed the events over and over again. I couldn't find one single thing I didn't like about the night, and I hadn't pushed it farther than she wanted me to go. I decided it was best to put it behind me. I had found with other break-ups that the best way to do that is to convince myself it would have never worked. Her lifestyle choices in no way mirrored my own, and I wanted to believe that one day I would be running a company, and I doubted she would fit in well at company parties. It wouldn't have worked. I was still disappointed, but then I thought about Victoria. She was still a very promising candidate; one that I had very much enjoyed getting to know. Life was not over, but the rejection was a bitch.

THIRTEEN

"I CAN'T BELIEVE HE IS doing this!" I woke up in a haze on the airplane. I had gotten in about two fifteen and laid there with my mind reeling until around three. Now I could barely see the light streaming through the windows, but I could hear someone, who was very angry, yelling in the other room.

"No, sir. I told him to meet me here at eight a.m. sharp, and he didn't show . . . What? He didn't come home last night? Uh! This is just like him!"

I was starting to take offense at her tone and frustration. I rolled out of bed in my boxers, and I didn't take the time to put pants on. I strode into the other room, my bare feet stomping against the hollow floor, to where I could see Beth pacing on the phone, and I could hear my father yelling out of the speaker.

"Who are we waiting for?" I said, resting my forearm on the wall. I squinted through the headache forming at my temples. Beth spun around gaping at my, err . . . wardrobe.

"You're here!" she squeaked. She gave me one long look up and down before her cheeks flushed a deep crimson red. I realized that my appearance could be a little startling, but the way she was berating me on the phone had pushed me past the thought of decency.

I could hear the voice on the phone asking, "What's going on, Beth?"

"Umm, I am sorry, sir. Drew is already here. I will let you know when we land. Okay. Yes, sir." She hung the phone up and pushed her long hair out of her face. "I didn't see you board the plane. Did you stay here last night?"

I nodded my head. She looked so embarrassed and I thought about trying to make it better, but then I remembered what she had so vehemently said, "*This is just like him!*" So I let her stutter and stammer trying to collect her words. I bit the inside of my cheek and said, "I guess I will head back to the bedroom and get dressed. Don't worry, I can find my way. I will just follow the stickers." I hoped she could hear the frustration in my voice. How dare she assume that she knew anything about me? I went back to the room and searched through my suitcase for the clothes I had packed for today. I went to slide one leg into my pants, and she appeared at the doorway. Hiding behind the doorframe, she didn't say anything at first. She stood watching me put each leg into my pants, looking away only when I stood to button them.

"What is it, Beth?" I gruffly said.

"I'm sorry, Drew. I am just really stressed out about this trip. Usually your father is here, and he handles it. His standards are so high that I am just . . . stressed."

I put on my shirt and was rearranging my tie for the third time when she walked over to me. "Here, let me." I let her. I had tied a tie a few million times, but my pride was wounded, and I could no longer focus on the mindless task.

Afterwards, she placed her hand on my face and rubbed my cheek. My first thought was that some of the cotton candy lip-gloss lingered on my cheek. My second thought was how soft her thumb felt caressing my rough cheek. "I promise not to underestimate you again . . . today." She winked. I smirked hoping that this wouldn't be an issue going forward. I had enough women putting me in my place here recently.

Beth left the room, and I went into the bathroom to comb my hair and brush my teeth. Beth hollered that we would be taking off soon, as if my hangover wasn't enough to deal with. I could still taste the fruity drinks from the night before, which at this moment were enough to make me sick. Putting on the darkest pair of sunglasses I owned, I sat down in the comfortable reclining chairs in the plane's living area. Beth plopped down in the chair next to me with a whole to do list for when we landed.

"Do you want to go over these now or?" she said. I held my hand up to stop her. I could already feel the plane easing into motion on the runway. I hated this part. The plane was turning around to line up on the runway. The stewardess passed by us after making the bed and readying the plane for takeoff. She buckled up in another room, and the plane sped down the runway before lifting off in the air. Beth could see the pure terror written across my face, and she reached her hand over and took mine.

She raked her thumb gently across the top of my knuckles, which actually seemed to help take my mind off it. I kept my hold on the armrest until the plane leveled out at probably a billion feet over the clouds. Beth was looking out the window, but I didn't dare to see what she was staring at.

"Okay, we can get started now." I had my hand covering my eyes so I didn't chance seeing the clouds rushing by the window.

She picked up on that and offered to close the shade which I happily agreed to. She stacked the papers in her lap, and we went over the itinerary for the weekend. The hours were long during the day, and there was one dinner on Saturday night we had to attend, but two of the days let out at six, which left us the evening to ourselves.

Beth's hair continued to fall down into her face and my hand ached to tuck it behind her ear. Until this moment I hadn't even glanced at what she was wearing. She had on a gray dress suit complete with a white button up collared shirt and those awesomely sexy black pumps. Her blonde hair was so straight it looked like she had taken an iron to it.

"I got a confirmation on the hotel reservations, so we should be good to go when we get there. They only had a suite left, but you will have your own room and bathroom." Beth winced as she waited for me to confirm it was okay. I had no problems with sharing a suite. In fact that was perfect.

The stewardess approached us about breakfast. She offered an array of juices, which induced the gag reflex in me. "Uhh, no thanks. Can you just bring us two bottles of water and some bagels?" I was in no shape to eat. I felt my stomach was traveling at a different speed than the rest of my body, but when she came back with the water, I heartily gulped it down. The assortment of bagels looked awesome; every flavor from sweet to savory.

Beth grabbed a blueberry bagel and smeared a huge dollop of cream cheese over it. She took a monstrous bite out of it, and I watched her wipe the cream cheese off the side of her lips. Her eyes almost crossed with ecstasy as she moved the sweet tasting bagel around in her mouth.

"Oh my gosh," she moaned. "You have got to try this." She held the bagel to my mouth, and I was a bit taken back that she wanted to share her food with me. I bit off a small corner, and she shoved the rest in her mouth.

"Mmm!" I responded. "That is delicious." It wasn't, but I enjoyed watching her eat and lick the remaining cream off her fingers.

"I know, right! I could eat these all day." She laughed. And what a beautiful laugh that was. I used this as my invite to ask some more personal questions. The flight would be over soon, and the rush of the day's events would make this trip a distant memory. I asked about her favorite foods and places to eat. I asked about her hobbies and things she has always wanted to do. Surprisingly our interests lined up more than we both realized.

We both loved history and museums and art. Neither of us liked heights, snakes, or any other life threatening hobbies. She was really into pool, which I found odd for many reasons. Her favorite food was seafood, and her favorite color was yellow. She responded in such depth that our conversation walked me all the way through the landing.

"All right, guys, I hope you have enjoyed your flight. I have been instructed to have this place looking immaculate for the "show and tell" tomorrow night. Please let me know if there is anything else I can get you." She was very pleasing. My mother had personally selected and trained our stewardess to ensure a pleasant experience.

We grabbed our things and loaded them up in the rented SUV. I let her drive as she was more familiar with the area. When we approached the conference center I was in awe. The traffic was backed up for blocks, but through the trees and stoplights I could see the modern metal building towering above. The rounded roof and the straight lines of the building were masterful. It was perfect for the convention, and I was excited to see the set up inside.

It was not disappointing.

Inside there were a variety of model aircrafts and sculptures of other travel devices like cars and trains lining the entryway. Planes hung from the ceiling on long metal cables, while mock set ups of a tank and fire trucks were strategically placed throughout the corridor. I was carrying a huge case containing the information for our table. We showed our badges to the deskman and followed the large crowd heading inside.

Beth had a copy of the building's layout, and she pinpointed Sloane Enterprises on the map. "Okay, we need to go here to set up. Then there is a meeting at eleven with the chairperson. We will break for lunch at noon and then the doors open at two." I nodded and smiled, before placing my hand on the small of her back. She jerked at my touch at first, but then settled back against my hand and let me guide her through the room.

Our booth was at the center of the "cul-de-sac" according to the map. Beth mentioned that my father insisted on being able to see the entire room from our table. When we arrived at the six-by-eight table, we immediately set to work putting up the boards and spreading out the flyers and pens. Beth had ordered a set of stress relief balls with our company logo plastered on the side.

Our theme this weekend was Rest and Relaxation Luxury Private Airlines! We, well mostly Beth, had played on the need to be pampered on flights. The crowd that we wanted to appeal to was the hardworking business men and women who needed to be able to escape and reach their destination in a timely fashion. My partner was busy putting everything just so, while I checked my hair and tie in the makeshift mirror I had stored in our bag. Appearances meant a lot here.

"You look so much like your father," she said. She didn't seem to say it from a place of malice, and I decided to take it as a compliment. "But you have so much of your mother's spirit in you." I had to agree. My mother and I were kindred spirits, both wanting to love and be loved in return.

"Thank you," I said because I could think of no other response. The clock was ticking, and we had to rush to get our seats for the meeting. The seats filled up quickly leaving only one corner seat in the very back. I motioned for her to sit while I was happy to stand behind her. Camera flashes clicked all over the center as Mr. Garman rose with his opening speech.

"Good Morning!" he shouted. "It is always such a pleasure for all of you to make the trip down here each year. I know Atlanta is always happy to host this event, and the staff here at Transportation Unlimited is full of wonderful people. Please give them all a hand!" The crowd erupted in applause before he continued. "Now we plan for this to be a safe, fun, and productive event. After our opening, we will break for lunch. I have listed some suggestions in your brochure, but you are welcome to make your way to any of the city's fine dining establishments. The doors will open at two p.m. sharp, so I suggest you be back at that time. Our tickets sold out almost immediately. There will be a few school age classes here on a field trip. I urge you to embrace them; not just as potential for your company, but as the future of our industry. I can look around the room and say with all certainty that we aren't getting any younger." The crowd exploded with laughter and a few "Speak for yourselves," could be heard from different corners of the room. Mr. Garman was a very enjoyable speaker, and I could remember him visiting my college graduation as a guest speaker. He spoke about going places in your life and how transportation could take you there. To this day I still feel like my dad put him up to it. He had been so set on me pursuing his dreams that he didn't want me to follow my own. "Enjoy your lunch everyone!" He exited the stage and the crowd began rushing for the exits. Beth was nearly trampled a few times. I pulled her out of the way and right into my arms. I let go immediately and half expecting her to move, but she stayed pressed up against me until the rushing crowd stopped.

"They must be really hungry," I joked.

"Men!" She laughed. "Whatever happened to chivalry?"

She was so close to me that I had this sudden undeniable urge to plant a soft kiss right on her forehead. Deciding against it, I offered her my arm, which she willingly took, and we headed out to the street.

"What would you like to eat?" I asked as Beth pulled out the map. "I wouldn't head down that street." I pointed to the swarm of people heading north towards the center square. They looked like ants scurrying around in their black suits.

"There is a burger joint down the street. I grabbed a bite there last year, and it was pretty good." I agreed and we headed to "Sal's Burgers and Beer" Sounded like my kind of place.

I had no idea that today's girls even ate burgers anymore. The fatty meat and the carb infested buns seemed to send girls screaming in the other direction. We were seated in a small booth in the corner. Beth ordered a bacon cheeseburger with all the fixin's and curly fries. I was a bit intimidated by her order. I ordered a Philly cheesesteak with sautéed mushrooms and onions and a side of chips. I had to fight the urge to grab a beer, but I could already feel the way Beth hesitated when I flipped to the craft beer menu.

Be responsible! I chided myself.

Beth was all business until the food arrived. We discussed how we would approach the companies about the show and tell and whether we could offer incentives to the buyers. When the food arrived, all conversation was shelved in favor of choking down the delectable sandwiches and sides in front of us. She had finished her burger and half of her fries before

I could finish the first half of my sub.

"I love burgers," she said.

"I can see that. You are starting to make me look bad here." She shrugged, licking some mayonnaise out of the corner of her mouth and slathered another fry in ketchup.

"Ehh, your sandwich was bigger." She winked and I nodded. At least she didn't take the opportunity to bash me like some other girls I knew. I tossed my napkin over the chips and pushed it away.

"That's it. No more food. I won't be able to stay awake for the presentation if I eat another bite." I stood up and swiped my card taking care of our lunch. She grabbed her bottled water, and we took our time strolling down the long streets back to the conference center. The buildings in this area seemed to reach all the way up to the clouds. I had one brief moment of insanity thinking about how it would feel to stand on the large balcony of the twenty plus story building next to me. Then I squashed that. *Uh, no thank you!*

We were the first ones back to the conference center and that gave us a few minutes to relax before we had to resume our business presentation.

Like a good worker, Beth was reporting back to my father on her phone. She had all good things to say of course, and my father seemed to have come off the ledge a bit from this morning. I laid my head back on the leather cushioned chair and dozed off to the sound of Beth's soothing voice.

"Oh, I hope you and Mrs. Sloane enjoy your vacation." She actually smiled when she spoke to my father, even over the phone. "Yes, you two have a great trip, and don't worry about a thing here. We have it covered."

FOURTEEN

I FELL BACK ON THE plush mattress in the hotel. The day had been exhausting starting with my long frustration filled night and with the sun setting outside my window, I wanted nothing more than to strip down and pass out in between the bed's cotton sheets.

Beth and I were sharing a suite on the top floor. I could see into her room from my spot on the bed. She was unpacking her suitcases and taking off her jacket. She removed her collared shirt revealing the white camisole underneath. I raised my head a bit to get a better look. I didn't want to get caught spying, but on the flip side she could shut the door if she felt under dressed. I couldn't help but admire her tan, toned body with all of the great assets she hid so well under the expensive suits.

She reached for the hem of her shirt and lifted it slightly before walking out of view. *Damn!* I thought. *When did I become a peeping Tom?*

She emerged a few moments later in a swimsuit that made the olive green one at my parents' look like a beach towel. I almost fell off the bed watching her saunter towards me.

"Whoa," I whispered.

"What?" she said. She looked down to make sure everything was covered. The bright pink triangles barely covered the round fullness of the flesh underneath. "You like?" she said spinning around. The back of the suit has a set of pink ruffles that completely set off my manhood sirens.

"Hell yeah! I like that. You look hot, Beth. Where are you headed in that?" I must have looked like that crazy cartoon character with my heart beating out of my chest. She was obviously amused with my response. Maybe amused wasn't the right word. She looked pleased with herself.

"Actually I thought it would be cool to head down to the pool for a swim or maybe get in the hot tub?" She pushed her hands through her hair to put it up into a high ponytail.

"I don't know if it's a good idea for you to go by yourself. You might get kidnapped looking like that. I know if I saw you it would be my mission to take you home." I instantly regretted my comment. *Okay, slick!* I said to myself. *Stop drooling and start playing hard to get before she kicks you to the curb.* My inner monologue was off the charts. It appeared that my body was struggling with how to handle this chick.

"Are you saying that you want to come with me?" She twisted her body from one leg to the other.

"I'm saying that you definitely shouldn't go by yourself, and since I am your escort to this event, I think it's the gentlemanly thing to do to accompany you." I mentally patted myself on the back. *Good one, Drew!*

She responded with a simple okay, and I jumped up to grab my trunks and get changed. I had never seen Beth like this. This fun flirty side was very appealing, and I wanted to follow her lead *wherever* she wanted to take me. If you had seen us a few days ago you would have thought I was her lowly servant, but now we might be confused as a couple traveling down to the pool. I stopped to grab a beer for me at the hotel bar, and Beth hollered to grab her a glass of wine.

I was only gone for two seconds before the pack of dogs sitting around the pool started howling at my, err . . . business partner. I had to force myself to take one step at a time even though I almost broke out into a run to catch up with her, but then I heard her speak. She didn't sound intimidated or mad, instead she said, "All right, guys, thanks a lot, but I am taken."

You could hear the "boos" echo from across the pool. I rounded the corner with our drinks, and Beth was nowhere to be seen. A moment of panic threatened to rise up into my throat, but then she emerged from the crystal blue pool water. The guys around the pool still couldn't keep their eyes off her. She plunged back underwater and swam towards me; her pink ruffles shimmered and waved through the water creating a delicate ripple of light.

She burst through the water, climbing the metal ladder to get out of the pool. I tossed her a towel, making every attempt to hide the goods from the competition across the pool. She sat down in the chair next to me and thanked me for the wine. She looked so relaxed just hanging out by the pool.

"How's the water?" I asked. She was still sipping her wine so I made a statement that came from a purely jealous place. "You seem to have created quite the fan club over there."

She snapped her head to the guys stupidly waving from across the pool. She almost spit out her wine when one guy stuck his tongue out and wiggled it around.

"Disgusting!" She laughed. I tossed back the beer and chugged it heavily. "Are you getting in?"

"Nah, I was thinking about the hot tub, but I think it is hot enough in here." I couldn't bring myself to get over the five douche bags sitting in the corner even though she was visibly disappointed.

"Okay, well, you can go back upstairs if you want. They don't scare me." She made her best attempt at perky, but I could see that she was upset.

"I am going to grab another beer, and then I will get in if you want, okay?" She had a sweet smile. I felt like a jerk, but maybe I could make it up to her. I hurried to the bar and back in record time. Beth was already submerged in the hot tub. Even through the bubbling surface I could see her perfectly curved body under the water. I took the steps into the hot tub one at a time trying to get used to the scalding hot water.

"You just have to walk in." she winked. "Hot water does amazing things for your muscles and your stress. Well, it does for me anyway."

Sitting against the slippery tile wall, I stared into the face of the beautiful girl across from me. "You were awesome today, Beth. My father would be very impressed with you, and so am I." I meant every word, and I wasn't sure why it came up then, but whenever I was around her I felt more like the person I should be.

"You did great yourself. We make a great team, Drew." She put her hand up, giving me a high five from her seat across from me. I felt silly high fiving this beautiful woman's hand in a hot tub when I wanted nothing more than to take her into my arms.

We stayed in the hot tub for a less than an hour. One of the guys decided it would be cool to cannonball into the pool next to us. The freezing cold water dumped on us chilling me to the core. I was sure that Beth was going to be upset, but being the diplomatic easygoing person she was, she simply thanked the guy for cooling us off.

We headed upstairs huddled in towels and when we got to our suite, I wrapped her up in the warm fuzzy robes hanging in my bathroom. We both took a shower, alone unfortunately, and got ready for dinner.

When she emerged from the bathroom, she looked lovely in a gray and white striped cotton dress. Her hair hung in loose curls, still wet from the shower.

I let her pick the restaurant the first night. She asked if I wanted to eat at the hotel, which triggered a flash memory of Claire sending out those delectable courses. I told her that we should try somewhere we had never eaten at before. She picked a restaurant that specialized in sushi. I was stoked to try out something new. I'd had sushi many times, but the flavors varied place to place.

Dinner was full of conversation, and we somehow managed not to talk about work. She talked about growing up in a smaller town. She was into a lot of competitive sports and gymnastics. I told her I used to play soccer in grade school, but by the time I made it to college, the only thing I played was beer pong. We laughed at stories about my dad's flying and how he was probably sitting on a beach somewhere checking the weather patterns.

"Your mom is a very classy lady. I think I will have to come over for dinner more often on Sundays," she said as I shoved another piece of tuna sashimi in my mouth.

I swallowed the mushy fish quickly and responded saying, "I'd like that a lot." I had gotten wrapped up in talking to her, and it wasn't until she looked at me with a sideways smile that I realized I needed to back track or expose my feelings for her. "My mother, I mean. She would like that a lot and I like it when she likes things . . ." *Epic failure.* I couldn't help it. I was sitting there with this beautiful woman hating myself for not being able to control my words.

We ended up back at the hotel around eleven. Neither of us could stay awake another second. The convention center was opening at nine the next morning. I said goodnight and headed to my bedroom. I wasn't sure whether to shut the door, and I teetered on the feeling that I should somehow tuck her in.

Maybe another time. Hopefully soon.

FIFTEEN

BETH AND I HAD BEEN on our feet meeting and greeting and repeating the same lines over and over again for the last six hours. We had even had lunch delivered to our booth because so many people lined up to speak with us. My father would call that a success, but I called it the recipe for exhaustion.

We still had over an hour left of touring the plane, and then we had to haul ass back to the hotel to change for the catered dinner that evening at the convention center.

Graciously pointing out the oversized restroom with the warming toilet seats to the umpteenth person, Beth shot me a look that said '*shoot me now.*' I put my finger to my temple pulled the trigger, letting her know I felt her pain.

"Mr. Sloane!" I turned quickly to find an elderly couple waiting expectantly behind me. "See, Alfred, I told you that was his son. You are Wyatt's son, right? I have been telling my husband all day that you looked like him." I could barely squeeze in a nod before the couple started bickering between themselves.

"Well Margaret, I never said the boy didn't look like his father. I said I couldn't believe that Wyatt would miss the conference. He hasn't missed one in the last decade." The old man's dentures rocked when he talked, and you could tell by the way he was yelling that his hearing wasn't the best.

"I had that same thought myself," I jolted in. "It shocked me very much when my father asked me to come in his place, but I am happy to be here and I hope you will consider doing business with us in the future." I shook both of their hands.

"Why yes, son! We have used your company many times in the last few years. I must say this plane is a beauty. I might just rent this to fly around sometime."

"We can certainly accommodate you. I must get back to the others, but it was a pleasure meeting you."

I joined Beth in the sitting area. She was slumped down in the recliner, and I fell into the one next to her. "I think that was the last of them."

Beth held up on limp hand and said, "High five, we did it." Our hands slapped together with our exhausted fingers entwining and resting together on the armrest. I had every intention of letting her hand go after our awkward handshake, high five thing, but this felt comfortable. "If I have to say the word *luxury* one more time I might die." She giggled.

"I feel ya," I said, huffing through the exhaustion. "Okay, pretty lady, we have to get back and get dressed before the ball this evening. Want me to help you up?" I felt for her. The sky-high heels had to be hurting her feet by now, and the form-fitting suit couldn't be much better.

"Yes, sir," she said. I climbed out of the chair and extended my arm. She grabbed on tightly, and I pulled her up. Teetering on her feet, she rested her hand on my shoulder for support.

"Are you okay?" I said when she didn't immediately step away.

"Yeah, I am good right here for a minute." I could smell the perfume scent rising up from her hair, and the soft skin around her wrist felt smooth under my fingers. She jiggled her foot around and laughed that her toes were asleep. She bent to take off the heels she had been in all day and proclaimed, "I think I'll make the trip barefoot."

"Not a chance," I protested. "That runway is full of debris and rocks that might cut your feet . . . I'll carry you." I hoisted her up into my arms to carry her outside.

"You don't have to do this!"

"Yeah, but I want to. Do you have all your stuff?" I asked. She pointed to the counter where her small black handbag was laying. Her body molded so perfectly to mine that I could have carried her for miles just to avoid putting her down. But there was the ball and the hundreds of hands we had to shake. The ride back to the hotel was slow with afternoon traffic backed up for miles. Beth rested her head on my shoulder as I navigated the narrow streets leading to the hotel.

When we arrived, I made sure she was okay to walk inside. She wasn't very happy about trading one set of heels for another, so I suggested that maybe a shower and a foot massage were in order. She headed into her room, and I retreated to mine. I got ready in record time. My tuxedo was perfect, and I had my shoes shined before I left. I slicked back my hair and sprayed on my favorite cologne before heading into the sitting area. I could see the steam pouring out of Beth's bathroom, and I was worried that she wouldn't make it out in time to leave.

I turned on the TV looking for some kind of distraction and about twenty minutes later, Beth appeared out of her room wearing the sexiest dress I had ever seen. It was an ivory colored dress with a black lace overlay. It had a low cut V-neck and a slit that left me wanting to rip it off her. She had a large set of dangly earrings and a chunky black necklace. Her shoes made her almost as tall as I was, and her blonde hair was wavy with thick curls. I vowed that she must want me as much as I wanted her to be wearing dresses like that.

"You look . . ." I tried to think of the best word to follow that up with like freaking sexy, hot, amazing, like a goddess. My mind rolled through all the descriptive words rolling around in my head. "You look exquisite,

Beth."

She smiled and said, "So do you."

We had a limo pick us up to drive to the event that evening. Beth and I were starving by the time we sat for dinner. At our table were three sets of representatives, the Minshaws from Wisconsin, the managers from Carter Transport in Florida, and the Waylons from North Carolina. The Waylons were the first to introduce themselves as longtime clients of our company, as well as, personal friends of my parents.' I was thankful that Beth knew them because I had no idea who they were. She managed to keep the conversation away from me by explaining why my parents weren't able to make it. They asked me a few questions about my "position" in the company and if I was ready to take over when he retired.

"I don't think my father will ever retire, he is practically immortal." The whole table erupted in laughter, and I checked that off as a dodged bullet. I hated the feeling that I may never live up to my dad's expectations, and I didn't know if I wanted to tie myself down to a field I didn't love for the rest of my life.

Beth must have sensed my mood change because she reached under the table and squeezed my hand lightly. I held onto it for a moment too long and the Carter Transport representative caught on. "Oh, so are you a couple?" I had no doubt he wanted to know if Beth was available. I didn't want to answer with anything other than "Yes, we are!" I wanted to stake my claim to this beautiful woman, but the truth was that she wasn't mine and might not ever want to be. So I waited with my eyebrows raised looking at the guy like he had three heads.

Beth removed her hand from mine and said "No. But Drew and I are a force to be reckoned with, and we are here to promote Sloane Enterprises." Good answer, but not good enough to keep the wolves at bay.

"We can see that," the man responded. He and his partner who appeared to be his brother smiled with cat-like grins as if they had just acquired their next target. Thankfully, the Minshaws joined in to talk about the change in weather from their state to ours. They hated the super-hot weather and preferred to spend their time in the mountains or in Canada.

Dinner was served moments later. The *transportation* theme was very predictable. The first course of three was a tray of things you might find if you traveled by boat. There was an array of bite sized seafood dishes and a bubbling cup of seafood chowder. Beth and I dug into the food like we hadn't eaten in days. I was grateful to be able to avert my attention to the food, instead of focusing on how badly I wanted to punch the other guy in the face for ogling that my, err . . . *partner.*

A speaker walked up and gave a very short, but sweet breakdown of the night's events. They thanked everyone for coming and blah blah blah. Another four speakers came up and gave their personal accounts of traveling and how important it was to find a company you like and to stick with them.

Sloane Enterprises was named in the top ten list of private providers, and we both stood to be recognized when our company's name was called. I could see the eyes popping out of the Carter boy's face, and when I looked to see what had him so captivated, I could see that the slit in Beth's skirt was flashing quite a bit of the tan flesh peeking out from the sequined material.

I shot him a disapproving glance and hoped that he would keep his eyes to himself. Seemingly completely oblivious to the attention, Beth sat back down and started in on her main course. The rather larger addition focused on what you might find if you traveled by car. They provided a thinly pounded skirt steak stuffed with sautéed vegetables and goat cheese rolled into a tight pinwheel. The sides included steamed vegetables and a stuffed baked potato.

The convention center had commissioned a string quartet to play during dinner. The soft rhythm was calming to my already confused inner dialogue. I had always enjoyed the violin and other classical music instruments. A few others were getting up to dance, and I could see the Carter boy adjusting his collar and smoothing his pants. I didn't want to risk him asking her first and her being too nice to say no.

"Would you join me for a dance?" I spit out the words so quickly I think she almost choked on the food in her mouth. "When you are done, I mean," I recovered, hoping she wouldn't find me rude for interrupting her meal.

"No," she said, wiping her mouth. "I'm finished, if you would like to dance?"

The abrasive Carter boy tossed his napkin on his plate and excused himself. *Yeah, punk, move along. You won't lay a hand on her if I can help it.*

I led her to the dance floor, and we began spinning and gliding around the wooden stage in unison. At one point, a slower song came on and Beth laid her head on my shoulder. The inner struggle I was fighting was becoming unbearable. I no longer knew how to respond or what to say. I wanted to tell her how crazy she was making me, but I couldn't let go of my father's warning not to mess things up.

"I could stay like this for a long time," she said into my chest.

"Me too." It was a simple response, but the look she gave me was a look of yearning and passion. I forced my head to stay in place, not to kiss her or make any moves that we both might regret. Our feet continued to move in circles, but neither of us could break the stare. I wanted her permission. I needed it. "You are the prettiest woman here." I meant every word. All the charm and the easygoing comebacks had drifted away the moment she shared that blueberry bagel the day before, leaving only a passionate and consuming urge. I wanted to make her mine.

"Kiss me, Drew."

"Are you sure?" I only questioned her to make sure that she had actually said the words and it wasn't just my imagination playing tricks on me.

She sucked her bottom lip between her teeth, but didn't answer. Dropping her hands and rushing off the dance floor, she fled from the banquet hall into the corridor. Following her from the room, I didn't know what to think. The corridor was not lit up, and although I could still hear the chatter from inside, the hallway was void of any people.

"Beth!" I yelled in a whispered voice. "Where are you going?" She was practically jogging in her heels as they clicked down the marble hallway. She abruptly stopped spotting a door to her left. She jiggled the handle which easily opened. I had no idea where this door led, but I was willing to follow this chick anywhere.

Once inside the pitch-black room, she reached for my hand and pulled me close. My mind was swirling, and I couldn't quite grasp the reality of the situation until I felt her lips meet mine. I was leaned against a cold, steel wall and her body was pressed against mine.

The warm, sensual kiss seemed to go on for days, and I was happy to be lost in it. When she pulled back a little, I ran my hand through her silky hair. "I have wanted to do that for a while now," she whispered.

I rubbed my thumb across her swollen lips, and in the quiet darkness, I could hear her shallow breathing. I leaned in and the sweet smell of her hair crept into my nose. Pulling out my cell phone, I shined the light around looking for any furniture. There was a steel information desk sitting a few feet away with some leather chairs around it.

I picked her up on the tall desk bringing us face to face. "You look so beautiful tonight, Beth. I have been trying to hold back, but I don't know if I can . . ." I ran my hand up the slit leading up her leg. "And this dress isn't helping my self-control."

"Is that a good thing?" She giggled.

"Well, that depends . . . on your expectations for this evening."

"What do you mean?" All hint of laughter had left her throat; instead there was a raspy voice.

"It depends on whether you want me as much as I want you and all that comes with that."

"I do," she breathed.

I didn't second guess her answer this time.

Our kiss lingered on my lips even when her lips had moved on to my neck. My hands caressed her lower back and butt. I pulled her closer to me, and I heard her breath exhale from her body. I was totally digging the soft biting and sucking she was doing on my neck. I could barely take much more of this teasing and the way she had been working me up for the last few days I was ready for some release.

"Beth, I want you right here," I said in a deep voice I barely recognized.

I couldn't see her face or whether she was nodding, but when she spoke, I could tell that she was mulling the idea over in her head. "I want you too."

That was all I needed to know. I spun her around and gently laid her down on the desk. She screeched out when her back touched the cold metal, but she quickly hushed herself. I was thankful for the high slit in her dress, which allowed me easy access to the smooth flesh beneath. I slipped her panties to the side and undid my pants. I ripped the foil packet I kept in my wallet and pulled her legs around my hips.

I leaned over her and kissed her deeply. "Are you ready?" I felt like a high school kid getting it on after a dance; it was exhilarating.

"Yes!" she breathed out. I slid inside her and let myself focus on the soft velvety skin. Beth let out the sexiest moan, and I struggled to keep my focus off the growing urge to explode. Her sequined dress scratched and scraped my arm giving me some sort of distraction, but even that seemed to exasperate the sensation flowing through me. I longed to see her face as I thrust my way to ecstasy.

Damn, she felt good.

I was getting so close, but I wanted to feel her go first. Her legs climbed higher and higher up my torso until they were neatly tucked beneath my arms. The soft moans had turned into focused ahhs, and then her body tensed up beneath me.

"Yes!" she yelled way too loud. I did the only thing I could think of to keep her quiet. I covered her mouth with my own. She arched and writhed towards me. Our lips smashed together, and I felt the slow burn rise up in my stomach. She wrapped her fingers around my arms and squeezed. When I finally let go, I could barely breathe through the waves of ecstasy. I held on to her shoulders, still buried inside her. I didn't want to move. I didn't want the connection between us to end, but we couldn't risk being caught in a public place. I kissed her forehead, and we both got up to put ourselves together; proving to be a daunting task in the pitch black darkness. I snuck out of the room first, and Beth slowly followed. We made a mad dash to the restrooms on the other end of the hall.

I stood in the hallway outside the bathrooms and waited for her to come out. She was still adjusting her dress and the redness in her cheeks was a continuous reminder that *it* just happened. I hadn't dreamed it or imagined that. Only a few moments earlier I was buried deep inside her.

My smile was plastered on my face, although she seemed more relaxed and a bit dazed. People were beginning to leave the conference room, and we fell in line following them out.

I felt a tap on my shoulder as we ascended the concrete stairs. "Where did you two run off to?" Beth grasped onto my arm as I spun around ready to face the arrogant prick from Carter Transportation.

"And why would you think that is any of your business?" I crossed my arms and watched as he tossed up his hands, stumbling over the stairs.

The smell of alcohol permeated with each word as he muttered, "This fine lady owes me a dance." Turning away from me, he set his smoldering eyes on Beth.

"I don't think the lady owes you anything. You should go sleep it off. Have a good night, Carter." Beth and I turned to walk away hoping to avoid any more confrontation, but the sorely rejected Carter wasn't planning to take *no* for an answer.

"Why don't you stay out of it, pretty boy? Come on, honey, you should dance with a real man," Carter slurred, pulling Beth's arm right out of mine. I spun around completely ready to punch him, but Beth beat me to it. Without a word of warning she turned, her hand connecting with his cheek in an epic slap. The stinging blow across his face echoed through the steel and concrete entranceway. A dozen or so patrons turned to witness the assault and a very stunned, very embarrassed Carter boy only shook his head before retreating to his SUV.

"Beth, are you all right?" I pulled her close. Okay, it was an excuse to pull her into my arms. She had already kicked ass, and I knew that she could handle herself.

"Yeah . . . let's just get out of here." Our limousine pulled up, and we hurried inside.

Once in the safety of the car, we were free to snuggle up close together. With her forehead on my shoulder, I held her in my arms for a moment. "There is something about you, Beth. I would like to get to know you better. I want to know everything."

"I am just worried about how that would affect my job, Drew. What if it didn't work out and you wanted me gone? I can't risk losing my job."

"You know you are a bigger asset to that company than I will ever be. If anyone left, it would be me, but I don't see that happening. We are both adults, and we could go into this with both eyes open. I feel something for you."

The elevator ride and the walk to the room were agonizingly long and as soon as we made it through the doors, her lips met mine, and I didn't let her go for the rest of the night. She fell asleep in my arms, and I was completely infatuated with the way that felt.

SIXTEEN

THE TRIP WAS OVER, but the way I felt about Beth was anchored deep within me. Even the plane ride home was almost bearable. We hadn't touched on the topic of how life would be when we got home, but joining the mile high club in the "luxury" king sized bed was all the confirmation I needed that things were all good between us. Beth checked off everything on my list, even some things I hadn't seen at first glance.

We had done our best to conceal our smiles when asked why we dipped out so early. Beth had feigned an illness, too much champagne maybe. *Yeah, something like that.*

She was anxious to get back home when we landed, and I could use a break to deal with the events over the last few days.

"So I'll see you tomorrow?" I said in between kisses as we stood hand in hand at the entrance of the plane.

"Yeah." She smiled. "Tomorrow."

One long lingering kiss later, I was headed off the runway, dragging my suitcases to the parking lot. Beth had stayed behind to go over instructions with the pilot, and I was waving like a fool at the empty plane. My cheeks hurt from smiling so much, and the only thing on my mind was a selfish wish that I could fast forward to the next moment she would be in my arms.

I tossed my keys on the dresser and stripped down to my boxers. I flopped down on the bed and checked my email. There were two emails waiting for me. The first was a follow-up with Victoria. She was going on about how nice it was to meet me and how I should contact her if I wanted to see her again sometime. The other was from a new girl, well one I hadn't recognized. Her name was Georgia, and she claimed to be a cowgirl. Her profile said that she was the daughter of a horse farmer and animals were her passion.

Her message said, "Hi Drew, I'm sorry my message was so late. This season is always busy for us with the shows and all. I'd love to meet ya sometime. You could come out to see the farm or maybe I could meet you in the city. Alrighty see you soon!"

I could hear the country accent in her words, and it was very charming. There wasn't a single regret when I deleted the emails. I did hate leaving Victoria after such a nice first meeting, but I couldn't imagine not seeing where this thing with Beth was going.

We had planned to have lunch the next day at work. I grabbed my phone and spent the next few seconds flipping through the pictures we had snapped during the conference. Beth in that outrageous bikini, and Beth in the jaw dropping banquet dress, and then there was my favorite . . . Beth sleeping on my shoulder in the massive hotel bed. I fought the urge to call her to see what she was up to. I wanted to know if she was feeling anywhere near as eager as I was. I didn't want to spend a moment away from her, but I didn't want to come across as the hormonal teenager I had channeled over the last few days, so I decided to call my buddy Matt. It had been weeks since we'd hung out, and I was curious to see what he would think about my progress.

"Hey man! What are you up to? I said.

"Nothing, just chillin' at the house." He sounded bored out of his mind.

"You wanna hang out? You could come to my place or we could head out?"

He opted for my place. There was plenty to do here anyway—pool table, hot tub, fully stocked bar. He had crashed here so many times I couldn't keep track. In fact, he lived in the guest bedroom for about a year after college.

Matt was the terminal bachelor type. He dated, sure, but he hadn't found the one and swore he never would. Matt said he would pick up Jason on the way. It would be a makeshift boys' night. Man, I was getting old.

When they arrived with a couple boxes of pizza, I instantly felt better. Beth wasn't far from my mind, but I could focus on something else, anything else. After a few rounds of pool and several alcoholic beverages, we got down to business.

"So Drew . . ." Matt slurred. "How has your online dating thing working out?"

"Oh man, are you on one of those?" Jason laughed.

"Yeah, I mean I was, but I think I found the one." We all high fived and the guys were dying to hear about this broken road. I pulled up my profile and received a few elbows and jokes about my answers. But when I showed them the girls I had been dating, they shut up real fast.

"Damn!" they said in unison when we got to Jenna's picture. "Please tell me she's the one."

"Nah! Not even close." I took a swig of beer and continued down. I gave them the breakdown of my dates. They thought the rave chick was super-hot. I may not have mentioned that she sent me packing, but that's not important.

When Matt got to Victoria, he asked me about her. He bent down to look more closely at the screen, and even with her daughter in the picture, he didn't look deterred. "Dude, if she is not the one then I want to meet her." He was mesmerized. I told him what I knew about her, and he didn't seem the least bit worried about having a kid in his life. I didn't quite know how to tell her that she wasn't for me, but my friend liked her. I decided to leave that to fate. He had her name and her profile information so he could contact her on the site and maybe it wouldn't be so awkward for her. By the end of the night, we were all still laughing and joking about me being Mr. Playboy.

"So Mr. Playboy, which one of these fine ladies is the 'one,'" Matt said, with one sleepy eye open.

"Her name is Beth." I murmured, with a dreamy *I'm in love* look on my face.

"Whoa, whoa. Beth? Like your dad's assistant Beth? Are you out of your mind?" Matt screeched, sitting straight up from his lying position on my couch. "Your dad is going to *freak!*" he sang.

"Yeah . . ." I agreed, as the wind was sucked from my chest. I took another swig of the room temperature beer and tossed it in the trash. "But it's cool, man." I tried desperately to reassure them, but really myself. Jason sat quietly staring into space as I continued, "I'll just have to convince him that I am serious."

"You can't help who you love, right?" Jason sputtered.

"Right."

Matt had passed out on the couch, and I was nearly asleep myself when Jason asked me, "How do you know that she is the one?"

That was a good question, and I thought for a moment about the answer. I didn't want to be all cliché with my response. Anyone could see that she was perfect, but I needed to say why she was perfect for me.

"She makes me want to be a better man." Simple, but true.

Jason seemed to buy that answer as well. He woke the sleeping, snoring, drooling giant up and drove him home. On the way out, Matt was muttering something about Jason being a great D.D., but Jason seemed like he was holding something back.

He opened his mouth several times to speak, but then he walked away. Curiosity got to me, and I approached him at the car after he dumped

Dopey into the seat. "Hey man, what's wrong?"

"Nothing, I just wanted to say I am happy for you, and I hope she feels the same way." He had said it with sincerity, but the words stung . . . a lot. It hadn't crossed my mind that after the wonderful trip we had that she could feel anything but love for me. But she had not said the words and neither had I. I wanted to make our relationship official, and I hoped she would agree to date me—officially.

Arriving at work twenty minutes early, I immediately went to check in with Beth. She wasn't there. I asked around and no one had seen her.

I was about to panic. I tried texting her, but no response. I waited expectantly in the hallway, but she was nowhere to be found. I tried to sit at my desk, but the suspense and worry ate at me. I barged into my father's office and demanded to know where she was.

"Sit down, son. I was hoping to speak with you this morning to discuss the reports coming in about the convention center expo. I am hearing very good things."

I hadn't come close to sitting down, and frankly, his stalling tactics were just exasperating my panic. "Yes, yes, Father, the numbers are great! Why isn't Beth here today?"

"Andrew, I don't understand what has you all riled up. Beth is merely taking a day off after a long weekend. She called in just this morning." He was sitting forward in his chair now, watching me pace through the room. "What have you done, Andrew?"

I froze. His voice was so accusing that my first response was that he could go to hell.

"Nothing, Father. Beth and I had a great weekend, and you said for yourself the numbers are great." Who was I kidding? I couldn't even convince myself.

His eyes narrowed, and he rubbed his temples. "Please tell me you didn't do anything that might make her feel uncomfortable working here?

"I love her, Father." The words came blurting out like vomit, and I couldn't pull them in fast enough.

My father banged his fist on the desk and began hollering obscenities on my direction. I could see the heads popping over the cubicles through the glass walls.

"Andrew, you never learn. You can't look past your own ego long enough to make a good decision. You go from a gold digger to a wholesome girl in one leap. Of course she wouldn't be in today. You have ruined the best thing about the company. And since my son doesn't see the importance of my company then I guess I'll have to live forever to keep it going. Now get out of my sight, you are dismissed for the day."

I stormed out of the office and past the leering wide eyes of the staff. I didn't bother signing out or any of my other duties. In fact, to hell with this place, I quit!

I passed my mother in the parking lot. I heard her yell, "Andrew, honey, what's wrong? Will you talk to me?"

All I could see was red. I hated myself for not stopping as my mother hurried through the garage after me, but I was too hyped up and heartbroken to stop and explain. I fired up the engine and roared out of the parking garage towards *somewhere*.

I drove for hours. I was mad at my father and confused about Beth. I didn't know what to think anymore. It appeared that I would be a terminal bachelor as well. I pulled into a gas station to fill up the tank. The sun was beginning to set and all the passing signs suggested I was heading to the beach.

By the time I reached the ocean, it was nightfall. The beach was empty minus some stragglers. I walked the shoreline for miles watching the waves rise and crash. I took another look at my phone . . . no messages. I relaxed on top of a sand dune. Even with the hot sun bearing down on the white grains of sand all day, when nighttime hit the sand was so cold it made your toes numb. I had removed my sandals, and I let the coldness seep into my feet.

I dug up a few broken seashells and tossed them back into the ocean. Maybe I was overreacting. Maybe Beth just needed a day to relax and collect her thoughts, but why hadn't she texted me? This was a classic sign that I was being avoided like the plague. I wanted to blame my father. The way he spoke to me made me feel like less than dirt. I regretted that I hadn't conquered my fears and followed in his footsteps, but why should I have to do that to earn his love and respect.

Now here I was sitting in the sand, watching the rise and fall of the waves—a man with a broken heart.

SEVENTEEN

I DIDN'T BOTHER CALLING out of work the next day. Let him dock my pay if he wanted. My phone had continuously rung all day, but it was my mother.

No calls or texts from Beth.

I rented a hotel for the next few evenings. I wasn't ready to leave the serene ocean to head back to the drama. My phone went off again at around lunchtime the next day. I answered more out of habit than anything. "Hello!"

"Oh Drew! Thank goodness you answered. Where are you?" my mother asked.

"I am a few hours away, what's wrong?""

"Your father feels horrible about what he said. He knows that you have been trying lately, and what he said was out of line."

"So why are you telling me instead of him?"

"Drew, your father loves you and he wants what's best for you, but the two of you are stubborn. Just come home and give him a chance."

Even if I wanted to give *him* a chance, I had no idea what to think about Beth. She basically disappeared on me. "Mom, it's not that easy."

"He told me about you and Beth. I don't know what happened exactly, but he said you love her. What happened down there?"

"Nah, I don't want to talk about it. It doesn't matter anymore. I will be home in a few days, but I doubt I will be returning to that company. Goodbye, Mother." I hung up before she could protest and before I could say something I would regret to the one person I could count on.

I spent the day walking from pier to pier looking at all the shops along the way. The beaches were crowded in the daytime with kids weaving and dodging in and out of the water. I saw a couple chasing each other into the water before stopping to kiss behind the waves.

This sucks! I walked back to the hotel and grabbed my things to head home. The long drive home was agonizing. I made several stops along the way because the overwhelming feeling of loss was settling in, leaving me restless and panicked. She was mine for such a short time, and I hated letting her go. I sent one more pleading text for her to contact me, but no response. I snuck in the house after dark. I had even put my car in neutral so it wouldn't be so loud when I pulled in.

The next morning I slept in. I vaguely remembered someone knocking on my door, but I was in no mood to talk. I got up around lunchtime and realized I didn't have anything else to do today since work was all I had been focusing on for weeks.

Dressed and ready to go with the darkest shades I could find, I walked through the doors at work and into my office. People were staring in awe at my arrival. I felt a sense of anonymity with the glasses on to hide the dark circles forming under my eyes. I knew they must be instant messaging each other because their fingers quickly set into motion.

I wanted to head straight to Beth's office, but I was hoping to fly under the radar until I had some kind of plan. There was a stack of files on my desk with a note to review them and make appointments. The same elementary task from before I did all this work to prove myself. No, this wouldn't work. I wanted to leave; I needed to leave this company and work somewhere I would be appreciated.

I threw myself back into my chair, just in time to see Beth rush by with her head down. She was avoiding me that much was true, but why? I was too exhausted to chase after her. She wasn't interested in talking, and frankly neither was I. In fact, I was coping the only way I knew how. I opened my email and pulled up Georgia's profile. Matt had told me that he and Victoria were talking, and I didn't want to get in the middle of all that so Georgia was the only one I hadn't been able to follow up with.

It was depressing that out of all of these girls I had no luck finding the one for me. I wasn't willing to settle long term, but the mood I was in threatened to make me desperate. I could tell that Georgia was online so I opted for an instant message.

"Hey Georgia, sorry I didn't get back to you sooner. I have been out of town on business for the last week. I would love to get together sometime when you are free."

"Sure thing, stud! I have a few things to tend to today, but I am free tomorrow afternoon, say about three thirty."

"Three thirty is perfect." I didn't give a damn about missing work or my father's threat to dock my pay. The only thing on my mind was to find someone who could numb the pain. I could still taste her lip-gloss, ya know. I could still feel the way that her hands grasped onto my shoulders, and I could still see her face when she was sleeping. What I couldn't do, however, was picture myself with any other woman. I hoped that feeling would subside with time. Maybe it was just the rejection wounding my pride or maybe she was the one that I was meant to be with. Either way I was doomed to be miserable without her.

That evening I heard my mother knocking on my bedroom door. I stayed silent avoiding the inevitable conversation for just a few days longer. She knew I was there, and she knocked several times before saying, "I am here if you need me." It wasn't my intention to punish her, but I couldn't get over the horrible things my father had said to me. I was already beginning to look for a new job. Obviously my father didn't need me since he was going to live forever. Jason owned an internet software company, and he had always talked about me coming on board as the marketing head to sell the products and make bids for contracts.

I emailed him saying we should get together soon to talk about the job offer, if it was still available. I could live without Beth. I just didn't want to.

I had already decided the night before I wouldn't be at work that day. So I spent most of my morning with Jason and his co-owner, Seth, talking about specifics of the job. The pay wasn't great since it was a startup company, but I wasn't really worried about the money. I gave them some marketing strategies and laid out my plan for the products. They seemed very impressed and said they would talk it over. I was happy to be making some progress in one area of my life. My father could no longer throw it in my face that he was supporting me. I had even considered moving out of their home to put some distance between us.

I left the house at two thirty and made the long drive out of the city to the address Georgia had provided. There was nothing but hayfields and gravel roads for miles leading up to her family's ranch. I hadn't seen country like this since my parents took me to North Dakota. The rolling hills of the wavy grains were already relaxing the anxiety I had towards meeting another girl that might break my heart.

When I pulled in the driveway, a whole flock of chickens flew up into the air. Scared the hell out of me. "What were things doing out of cages?" I wondered. From the corner of my eye, I could see someone trotting towards me. Georgia bounded off the porch and crossed the yard to me. She was wearing a tight pair of denim jeans with holes around the knees, a pair of cowboy boots, and a red plaid sleeveless shirt that was tied above her belly button. *Hello, sexy!* I thought.

"Hi, I'm Drew. It's nice to meet you." I held out my hand, but she flew into my arms for a hello hug.

"Hey there, handsome! I'm glad you were able to find us out here." She turned her attention to my car and started screaming, "Whoa, look at this ride! A Nova, right? Can I sit in it?"

"Yes, ma'am!" It was cool that she liked the car; some girls, including Camille, preferred something a little less "noisy" and a little more "classy."

She sat down in the driver's seat and gushed about the original leather seats and radio. She shut the door and said, "How do I look?" She turned her head to the side and posed.

"Very hot," I said. "Do you want to drive it?"

"Do I ever! Get in, cowboy!" I got in, but when she started the motor and revved the engine I got a little nervous about where she might be headed.

"Do you mind if I get her dirty?"

"Not at all." I had no idea what was in store, but a little dirt wouldn't hurt anyone. She took off through the front yard and into the field behind it. She pressed her foot on the gas and the car bounced and spun through the never-ending field. She slung the car to the right, and we slid sideways a few feet before she gunned the gas and we shot off in the other direction. My heart was pounding, but I had to admit this was fun; like four wheeling with a cage around you. She made a few more loops around the field before parking it back in its original spot in the front yard.

"Wow! Where did you learn to drive like that?" I was genuinely smiling for the first time in days.

"Well, I ride horses in the rodeo, and I guess driving tractors and trucks around here in the snow had something to do with it. I have four older brothers, and they are always horsin' around."

"Oh no! Four older brothers, huh? Sounds like I need to be careful." It was kind of intimidating to think about not only having to impress parents, but brothers too.

"Well that depends, city boy. Depends on what your intentions are with me." Her country accent and attire made her adorably cute. We laughed and joked for a while before she invited me to "sit on her porch and drink some lemonade." I gladly joined her looking for any kind of distraction. Sometimes I felt like I was looking through her when she spoke. Beth hadn't quite vanished from my mind, and even through all of Georgia's charm, I wasn't ready to let that go.

"Well Ms. Georgia, what all do you do on this farm?" I sipped the sour lemonade and tried not to make a face at the tang that followed.

"I tend to the horses mostly. The boys do most of the mowing and hay baling. I teach a riding class on Saturday mornings, and sometimes I go to horse shows or to the market on Saturday afternoons."

"I have never ridden a horse actually. Think you could teach this city boy how to ride?" I wasn't sure if she would take that wrong, but it did sound a little dirty coming out of my mouth.

"Well, let's find out." Georgia reached for my hand and dragged me to the stables where she introduced me to Starlight, a black coated mare with white spots resembling a sky full of stars on her back and sides. "Starlight is my best starter horse. She doesn't go anywhere I don't tell her to."

The horse was already saddled and Georgia said, "Just hop on up there." I was glad that I wore shorts because I would have certainly ripped my designer jeans trying to climb up on this giant horse. "I can get you a step stool, if you want?"

"Nah, I think I got it." I didn't. My foot slipped out of those stirrup things a few times before I managed to swing my arm up grabbing the saddle horn. I pulled myself up on top of the horse, holding on for dear life. I didn't like how high I was off the ground sitting on the massive beast.

"That's right. You got it. Now hang on, I am going to walk you out." She pulled the rope and Starlight began to move forward. "Don't forget to duck!" I narrowly missed the barn door rafter on my way out.

"Whew! Now pick up the rope and pull to the left." When I did as she asked the horse turned her head and went in the direction I was pulling. *Neat!* Then I pulled the back the other way and once again she turned.

"That is so cool," I said. I was mesmerized by the pure size of the animal and its ability to be trained to do something that may not be incredibly natural to it. It was very enlightening. When I compared it to my own life, I was forced to look at how I had rebelled against my father's company more out of pride than out of dislike for the company itself.

Georgia disappeared into the barn before emerging back into the open sunlight. This time she was accompanied by a light tan male horse. She said his name was Acorn, and he was her personal horse. She looked gorgeous sitting on the horse with the sun behind her.

"You ready to ride?" She winked my way.

I wasn't quite sure, but Starlight's gentle nature made me feel more comfortable. "Giddy up!" I laughed. She showed me how to get the horse moving by kicking my heels into her side. I didn't feel overly comfortable kicking the horse, but she assured me it wouldn't hurt her. We started in a slow trot across the field. We went down a pretty steep hill. Feeling uneasy with the angle we were traveling, I didn't release the air pent up into my chest until we reached the bottom. We came upon a creek bed in between two large hills, and she dismounted her horse, tying him to a tree. I did the same, and we walked along the creek line chatting about our lives.

She told me that she had never lived anywhere except at this ranch, and she couldn't imagine living in the city away from her horses. I wasn't sure how I felt about that, but the business opportunity I was working on with Jason's company only limited me to a place with internet access and cell service. I did have my doubts that this part of the countryside may not offer that.

Admittedly, that concern was a long ways away. I might enjoy the farm life after enough time passed. The sun began to set, and she said we should head back before it got dark. I climbed back on Starlight, which was a lot easier the second time. On the way back, Georgia kicked her horse and broke out into an all-out sprint. I followed behind and the horse took off across the meadow. It was completely exhilarating to be galloping through the tall grass with a beautiful woman leading the way.

We ended up back at the house, and we walked the horses back to their stalls.

"I had a wonderful time tonight. The horses are great, and you're a great teacher," I said, motioning to the stables behind me. The farm and the million acres surrounding it were pitch black once the sun went down.

"Oh no, city boy, it's not polite to let a guest go hungry. You are staying for dinner, besides all them brothers of mine will want to meet you." She grabbed my hand and took off before I could decline. *Hell, what else did I have to do other than have dinner with four protective brothers? Great.*

We walked into the house, and she yelled for them to come down for dinner. I could smell the floury biscuits baking in the oven, and there was a heaping pot of gravy simmering on the stove. "Hope you like biscuits and gravy."

"Yeah, sure. I'm starving." I wasn't.

I heard a rumbling and then one by one the boys lined up in the kitchen. They were followed by an older couple I assumed were her parents. Her parents looked weary with crinkles around their eyes and wrinkles on their hands. I reached out to shake the gentleman's hand first. He hesitated a bit, but then gave my hand a good strong grip.

"Hello, sir, I'm Drew. It's nice to meet you."

He only grunted in response, but her mother smacked him on the shoulder with her apple printed potholder and said, "Don't mind him. We don't have strangers out this way much. I'm Betty, and this is Charles. Well, you've met Georgia, and these are our boys—Nash, Stuart, Billy, and Garret. The boys looked younger than their sister. The oldest was maybe twenty at best and the youngest around nine years old.

I no longer felt the pang of intimidation in my chest. All the boys seemed pleasant and well mannered. Their mother asked them to set the table, and they all obeyed completing their individual job. I sat between Georgia and the oldest boy Nash. When supper was served, they said grace before digging into the food. Two heaping piles of biscuits were on each end of the table and a bowl that could have held a gallon of milk served as the gravy bowl. I had no idea what to expect when I followed suit, dumping a healthy serving size of gravy over two, large, made from scratch biscuits. They also served pieces of thick cut bacon with the meal.

"Oh my goodness," I said when I took my first bite. "Do you eat like this every day?"

His mother blushed a bit before responding, "Well, Mr . . . Drew, we are not in a habit of ordering out from way out here, so we cook breakfast, lunch, and dinner right here in this kitchen. All made from scratch and all fresh ingredients from the farm."

I was thoroughly impressed with the farm's efficiency. They really made the "original" American dream a reality. It was comparable to camping in the wilderness; just they did it every day. After supper, Betty served a plate of apple pie, which was so delicious I burnt my tongue eating the steaming hot filling too quickly.

Georgia's family consistently laughed and talked together, and I was envious of their relationship. My family was nowhere near this close, and I had to believe it was because of the lack of distractions out here.

I left that night with a slice of pie and a quick kiss on the cheek from Georgia. Even her father shook my hand on the way out saying I was welcome back anytime. The boys spilled out of the house, and Georgia was quick to brag about how she took my car for a ride. The boys barked about being jealous and said how cool it was. I started the engine and it roared to life pumping up the little guys even more.

Heading home that night I felt that a weight had been lifted off my spirit, but deep down I had this hole that ached in my chest. Something that wasn't likely to go away anytime soon.

EIGHTEEN

I RETURNED TO WORK on Monday more out of boredom than any-thing else. I didn't leave my office for a better part of the day. Georgia had messaged me a few times over the weekend, and I was quick to respond. She said that she would be fixing fences with her brothers all weekend, but might be available on Monday and that there would be some more of that pie.

Georgia's bubbly personality was contagious, and I was even excited about seeing her horses again. I pushed my computer to the side and start-ed working on the stack of potential clients. I made my way through the list and was done by lunch. I hadn't seen Beth walk by all day, and I won-dered if she was even here. I walked down the hallway and into the break room where the new vending machines had been installed. I heard the clicking of heels come in behind me.

"Oh," she said. "Hi Drew, I didn't know you were here." Her voice sounded shocked like I had caught her off guard for showing up to work.

"Would you have come in here if you had known?" There was a bit of irritation in my voice, but only because she had gone to such drastic lengths to ignore me after what was quite possibly the best three days of my life.

"It's not like that, Drew," she stumbled.

"Oh really? Well enlighten me." I set my newly opened bag of pretzels down and crossed my arms, waiting for the words I had deserved to hear days ago.

"It's not that simple. I just can't be with you . . ." She rushed out of the room and I was kicking myself for making her upset, but dammit why wouldn't she tell me what the problem was? Had I done or said something to change her mind?

I spent the rest of the day staring at the picture of us together at the convention center. She had a smile on her face, which I longed to see again. I wanted to put that smile on her face again, but there was something going on, and I didn't know how to fix something that she didn't feel comfortable telling me.

My office door popped open, and I shot my head up to look at the intruder. It was Maya, the office manager, and she spilled, "I just wanted to thank you for the changes in the office. It was a breath of fresh air in the office that the employees desperately needed, and we are all thankful for your hard work."

"You're more than welcome." I smiled.

That was probably the best thing I had heard in the last few days. I wasn't going to get that pat on the back from my father for sure. I left my office and headed to the elevator. Just when the doors went to close a hand shot into the elevator and the doors popped open again. It was Beth.

I could see that she regretted her decision already, but she got into the elevator anyway. I could smell the sweet scent of her hair from her side of the elevator. Stopping myself from reaching out to her was like torture.

When the doors opened she shot out like a bullet, and I couldn't resist saying, "Beth, wait!" She turned around to face me, but she was still several feet away. "Beth, you have to make me understand. What happened with us? I thought everything was good, and now you are avoiding me like the plague. I don't understand." I was pleading with her for some answers. A tear rolled down her cheek, and I closed the distance between us wiped the tear from her face. "Beth, talk to me. Whatever it is, we can get through it."

She shook her head and said, "No, Drew, we can't." I refused to let her walk away until I got some answers. She took a deep breath like she was ready to talk. What she said next was worse than I could have imagined. "Drew, I have a boyfriend. I can't date you because I am already with him."

My heart leaped into my throat, and I was void of any words. "That can't be true, Beth. Whoever he is, he can't make you feel the way I do." She started walking towards her car, and I had to jog to keep up.

"No, Drew! I just can't . . . I can't be with you. Whatever happened before was a *mistake*!" Her words echoed through my heart, and I stopped in my tracks.

I didn't move from my spot in the middle of the parking garage until another car approached and beeped their horn. I couldn't tell you how I made it home that day, and after a few drinks, I couldn't tell you where I was.

My mother knocked on my door again. This time I let her in. I wasn't really the crying type, but my mom sat and listened to my problems. She didn't comment or correct me until I was completely finished, and even then, she soothed that everything would work out in the end. She said she was very proud of me for putting myself out there and that I would make a woman very happy one day.

Even though I could have predicted that response a mile away, it still made me feel a little calmer and more at ease with the situation. I was definitely on a path to a hangover, but my mom brought me a glass of water and some aspirin. She didn't linger. I guess she could tell I needed my space.

The next morning I woke up to an email from Georgia. She said that she was making a trip into the city today to pick up some riding equipment and asked if I was available for lunch. I didn't bother going to work, instead I got dressed and went to meet Georgia at a farmers' market downtown.

She was in her typical attire—a pair of daisy duke shorts and a pink tank top with her cowboy hat on and her boots. We picked up a few sandwiches and sat down in the grass on the courtyard. I loved the way she was relaxed and could talk about anything without having to pry it out of her. We took a stroll around the market, and she showed me how to tell which vegetables to buy. I bought her a bag of cotton candy, and she was delighted to see how it melted on her tongue. She said that they worked seven days a week, and that on occasion they had gone to county fairs, but even then, they were busy selling produce or other baked goods. I told her that there was a fair a few counties over going on right now.

She was very excited when I asked if she might accompany me to the fair on Friday night. She said she couldn't stay out too late because she had so much work to do the next day. That was fine by me, and we set the date for Friday night.

When we parted ways, I went to meet Matt for drinks at Jimmy's. He greeted me with a high five, and I sat down to order a beer.

Matt was practically glowing, and I had a feeling it had something to do with Victoria. "Okay, man, spill it. What has you smiling so big?"

"It's her, man! Vic is a special lady, and the whole single mom thing doesn't even scare me. I talked to her on the phone a few times, and I heard Emmaline in the background. She seems like a cool kid. I could do cereal and Saturday morning cartoons. Besides that woman deserves someone who can support her. She works too hard."

He wasn't saying anything I didn't already know, but it was cool to know that Victoria would be taken care of. She did deserve the best kind of man, and Matt was one of those. I let him talk. He had listened to me babble on the other night, and I didn't want to mess up his moment.

"I can't believe we both found love. I mean look at us. A couple of bachelors who found beautiful, smart women to be with."

"Actually . . ." I said. "Beth and I aren't together. She just stopped talking to me and said that she has a boyfriend so we can't be together. How is it possible that she never mentioned this guy the whole time we were together? She said that what we had was a *mistake?*"

"Do you think she just made up the other guy thing just to throw you off?" We both took a swig of beer and I considered that as a possibility, but if she was willing to go through all that just to push me away maybe I was better off without her. She obviously wasn't worried about our relationship or me.

Matt looked crushed, and I felt like a douche for bringing him down. "It's cool though, man. I am talking to this new girl, and she seems pretty cool. Maybe it was meant to be like this."

Matt patted me on the back and hollered for the bartender to give us another beer. We changed the subject, of course, to my job dilemma. He understood why I would want to leave my father's company, but he gave me some wise words of wisdom that I wouldn't soon forget. He said, "Drew, if you start walking away from the hard stuff now, you will never stop."

Maybe so.

NINETEEN

I HAD MANAGED TO STAY away from Beth and avoid my father as well for the next week. I came in and did what was laid out for me and went home. Beth had so graciously begun putting all my files on my desk before I even arrived. *Thanks a lot.*

This afternoon Georgia had begged me to drive out to the ranch at lunch today. We were already planning to meet this afternoon to go to the fair a few counties over, but she said she had something to show me. I sped down the long dirt road, and when I approached the farmhouse, I could see a large school bus and around ten cars parked on the lawn. The side of the bus read, *Special Kids Network.* I had no idea what was going on, but Georgia had been awfully excited on the phone.

I walked down to the barn where I saw Starlight tied to the post all saddled up. I gave her a quick rub and walked to down to the ring. Georgia was in the middle of the ring holding leads of several horses. People were standing all around the ring watching while others were brushing the horses and feeding them with her brothers' help.

There were a few children in wheelchairs and others were being led by hand. I had heard of programs where children with special needs could interact with horses and how the animals could be soothing to them. Seeing Georgia interacting with the kids was magical. She was kind and patient, but didn't treat them like they were helpless. She guided them through the steps and encouraged them to take control, well as much control as they could handle.

A little boy named Austin came up to me and tugged on my shirt. His handler said that he was autistic and that he had refused to speak until they had begun coming to the ranch for lessons. Austin pointed at the horse and said, "Acorn!" Sure enough, that was the horse's name.

"That's right, Austin. Is he your favorite?"

The boy nodded and then ran back to pet the horse as it came to a stop. Georgia patted him on the head and lifted him up on the Acorn's back for his turn. The boy was noticeably excited. His handler continued to explain some of the challenges that the children faced and how equine therapy could improve motor skills, as well as, social and communication skills.

"The hardest part is finding funding and people who are willing to sponsor the programs. Georgia and her family are the only ones in the area that offer their services for free. The children love coming." The counselor let out a long sigh.

My heart ached for the kids and adults with special needs. "I never realized how hard life must be for them," I said.

"Unless you see it every day, it seems like such a rarity, but our country is filled with diversity. One in five Americans has some type of disability."

I wanted to help somehow, but I didn't know where to start. I spent a little time interacting with the kids before they got on the bus to head home. Georgia went to change her clothes to leave for the fair, and I spent the next few minutes sitting on the porch reviewing the day's events.

When Georgia emerged, I was completely taken aback. She was wearing a burgundy-colored frilly dress with a large purple flower across it, and she paired it with a newer pair of cowgirl boots. This was the first time

I had seen her without a cowboy hat. Her long brown hair hung down covering most of her back, and in the low sunlight, it sparkled with sun-streaked highlights.

"You look beautiful, Ms. Georgia." She smiled and did a little curtsy. We headed out to the car and began the hour-long drive to the county fair.

The weather was perfect for an evening outside, and we rode in a comfortable silence for most of the time. The fairgrounds were packed with cars as far as the eye could see. Georgia's eyes sparkled with joy when we approached the large Ferris wheel and the dozens of other carnival rides. Most of them were for kids mainly, but there were a few fun/scary rides.

She begged to ride the Ferris wheel, and at first, I objected. The thought of being that high up in the air was frightening, and I wasn't overly confident that the old rickety wheel wouldn't lead me to my doom, but Georgia insisted saying that she would hold my hand the whole way. She did just that. We climbed into one of the bucket seats, and I made sure to lock the bar in tight. We were forced to sit so close together that the only place I could put my arm was around her. She grasped onto my hand, and as we rode higher on the wheel, I kept my eyes on her. The lights in her eyes and the smile on her face making my gag-worthy fear all worthwhile.

Her country girl charm was very endearing. When we made it to the top she said, "Wow, it feels like we are a mile high in the air."

The words mile high created a flashback in my head of me and Beth rolling around in the luxury bed flying back from the convention. The pain and anguish I felt must have shown through on my face as Georgia seemed to catch on. She put her hands over mine and squeezed gently. I wanted so much to get past this misery, and Georgia was a great girl. She was honest and caring and very talented. She could teach me things I would never learn otherwise. Other than the Ferris wheel, she hadn't pressured me to do anything or feel a certain way. We were free to just hang out and get to know each other.

After the Ferris wheel ride, Georgia dragged me around the fairgrounds where we got a funnel cake and tried deep fried Oreos. *Gross.* We played every fair game there was and even won a goldfish for Georgia. Armed with a bag full of stuffed animals, we headed back to the car. We had almost pulled out when an explosion sounded in the air. The fair employees were shooting off fireworks to end the night. We sat there watching the fireworks, and I considered planting a kiss on that rosy peach cheek of hers, but I couldn't look at her and see someone I wanted to be with. There was only one girl that I wanted, and until I figured out what the hell was going on with her, I couldn't be with anyone else.

I drove Georgia home and she said, "I had a great time tonight. The fair was more magical than I could have dreamed. Have a good night, stud."

"Yeah, I had a great time." I smiled, handing her the bag of animals. I waited for her to get in the door to her house, and I started the long drive home. Tonight was great, but it also helped me realize who and what I really needed.

I sat in my driveway for an hour staring at the picture of Beth and me. Against my better judgment, I had made the picture my phone screensaver. I pulled up her number and started to text her, but stopped. I wasn't going to win her back with a text message.

It was almost ten o'clock when I walked into the living room in the main part of the house. My father was reading a newspaper in his chair, and my mother was watching a cooking show on TV. I approached them and declared my love for Beth. I told them that I was going to find a way to win her back and that I hoped I had their support in the matter.

I didn't know quite why I needed it, being that I was an adult, but the leading protestor between us was my father. He had not liked the idea of us being together from the beginning, but he had to understand that this was not a conquest of mine. "She is the first girl that makes me feel this way. I love her." My mother was smiling from ear to ear, and my father's face looked as if it would explode.

"You are such an arrogant child. What makes you think she wants *you*? A good girl like that, who is always on time and who makes work a priority, deserves someone with the same goals and aspirations. You have been such a disappointment, rebelling in every sense of the word, and now you want to corrupt my best employee."

"Wyatt, that is enough!" my mother yelled. "You will not speak to our *son* that way. He has proven himself in lots of ways, and I imagine that no one would want to work for a man who acted like such a tyrant all the time." She looked my father directly in the eyes and said, "Wyatt, they are adults, and they can choose to be with whoever makes them happy. You can't choose who you fall in love with, and I certainly don't expect them to ignore it."

I was happy that my mother understood and that she was standing up for me. My father relaxed in his chair a bit, but maintained the heated look on his face. "Father, I know you don't understand and I know that you don't think I deserve her, but we have something that you can't break."

"Oh really, son? Is that why she agreed to stay away from you?" He covered his mouth pulling at the mustache covering his lips and looked away.

"What are you talking about?" I couldn't shake the feeling that he was hiding something. "Wait! Did you say something to her? You said she agreed. Did you ask her to stay away from me?"

"Wyatt, please tell me you didn't." My mother was visibly upset.

"It's because it's me, isn't it? You would rather me be miserable than risk losing your assistant? Well, the joke's on you because this is going to make you lose us both."

I stormed from the room and headed straight to my bedroom. I heard my mother's footsteps coming behind me, but I didn't stop. "Andrew, your father doesn't mean it. He just doesn't understand how you two feel about each other." She continued to speak as I packed my clothes. "Don't leave, honey. Give it a few days and if you still want to leave I will help you look for a place."

"How can the people that you care about care so little about your feelings? I mean she agreed, Mother. She could have stood up for us and what we were creating together, but instead she walked away. He wouldn't have fired her if she chose me, so why would she so willingly give it away?" I wanted to scream, cry, and throw things. I couldn't put all of this on my father because she agreed to it.

"It wasn't my intention to hurt you, son." My father had snaked his way into my doorway before I had even realized it.

"What did you say to her, Father? Did you tell her that she would lose her job if she dated me? Did you say that I was some sort of womanizer or that I was too lazy or too selfish to deserve her? Or did she really decide on her own that I wasn't good enough? I need to know."

My father dropped his head and shuffled his feet a bit before saying, "If I would have known how much she meant to you . . . If I thought that you were serious, Drew, about any of this," he muttered, waving his hands. "Then maybe I wouldn't have said anything at all. But you have to understand that I have been trying to teach you and guide you to become a better man." My mother sank into the sofa and was rubbing her temples. "You haven't even tried to be the man you could be; the man that I *know* is in there."

"Just because I don't see things the same as you do does not make me weak or lesser in value than you. What would the world be like if we all thought the same? You would rather crush your son's dreams and force him to live your own. I am not just talking about Beth, Father, you have been pushing me away for years and replacing me with your business. What kind of man does that make you? At the end of the day all you have is a thriving business and a wife that is begging you to be with her and a son who can't stand to be around you." My voice had gone hoarse from all the yelling. The way he looked at me like he was shocked at what I said made me feel like he hadn't understood. My father walked away that night. My mother stood and hugged me before following after him.

I sat on my bed unable to sleep and too tired to pack. I wondered if Beth felt this horrible. My father never said what he and Beth had talked about. I lay with my arms behind my head and waited for the sun to rise. I thought all night about what to do. I had considered getting her address and storming into her house to profess my love or maybe following her into the parking lot before work. I wanted her to know that I could make sure she lived a happy life. To hell with my father and his unrealistic expectations. I just wanted her.

TWENTY

I ARRIVED TO WORK THIRTY minutes before any other employee. I waited at my office door for her to arrive, but as employee after employee arrived, there was no sign of Beth. I approached Catherine, with our collections staff, to ask if Beth was going to be in today.

"I know that she has a meeting with your father this morning, but she should be in later." She winced when she said the word "later." I wondered if everyone knew what was going on and was just too scared to say anything.

I thanked her and sent her on her way while silently cursing my father. There was no telling what he was saying to her now. I almost left to crash the meeting, but I had no idea where she would be. So I waited and waited, checking the clock every few minutes. Lunchtime rolled around, and I had almost fallen asleep when there was a light tap on the door.

I sat straight up fully expecting to see Beth. Instead in walked Camille. Her dress was so short you could almost see her butt hanging out of the back. I was not in the mood for a visit from her, and I made it known.

"Stop being so rude, Drew. I am only here to tell you thank you for what you did the other night. I was leaning back on my desk while she paced the room in front of me.

"Did you find a place to stay?" I asked.

"Actually I moved back in with my parents. They laid down the rules, and well, I have broken a few, *but* I have enrolled back into school. I was accepted into the nursing program. Isn't that wonderful?" She jumped into my arms, and I allowed myself a small hug before I pushed her back by the hips. She pushed against my hands, but I continued to hold her at arm's reach.

"Yes, that is wonderful, Camille. I am very happy for you, but today isn't a great day." I stood and walked over to the windows to put some distance between us, which she quickly closed.

"So does that mean that you and I might have a chance?"

I hated to break it to her and it was going to hurt us both, but like a Band-Aid, you had to rip it off quick. "Camille, I am in love with someone else. You and I are great friends, but that is it. I wish the best for you." I turned back to face the window, and she hugged me from behind. She kissed the back of my neck, and I heard a gasp. I spun around in time to see Beth fleeing from my office.

I froze. "I take it that was her, huh?" Camille spit it out with such disgust. "Kind of plain, if you ask me. I think you . . ." I didn't wait for the rest of the words to be spoken. I hurried out of my office and sprinted down the hall. She wasn't in her office or in the break room. I ran down to the parking garage, taking the stairs a flight at a time. I saw her car pulling away, and I jumped in front of it. She slammed on her brakes and put her head on the steering wheel.

I opened her car door and kneeled down next to her. "Drew, what are you thinking?"

"Beth, I have been waiting all day to see you."

"Well, it didn't look like you had to wait alone," she snarled.

"Camille was just here to thank me for some advice I gave her, that's all." I reached for her hand, but she quickly jerked it away.

"My father told me that he is the reason you have stayed away since we got back. Why would you give up on us?"

Beth was sobbing, and I could barely understand her words. I pulled her into my shoulder and held her there for a few moments. "He said that you only dated girls that you could use and that you liked the challenge, but that you were never serious. He said that you would ruin my career and break my heart in the process. And here you are proving him right. Please tell your father that I quit." With that, she pushed me backwards and shut the door. She drove off, and I sat on the cold dirty ground wondering how it was possible to fail at everything that mattered to me.

I heard footsteps crossing the garage. My father had undoubtedly heard everything we had said. He was wearing a three-piece suit that had been specially tailored for him, but when he reached my side, he sat down on the grimy oil stained concrete and for a moment, we sat in complete silence.

"You know, son, when I began this business I had two goals in mind. The first was that I could create a legacy for you and your mom. I wanted everything in life that wasn't available to me to be at your disposal. The second was to create a business surrounding all the things that I love and cherish the most. Somewhere that has gotten lost along the way."

I smeared a tear off my face and said, "Ya think."

Sounding defeated, my father chuckled and said, "Yeah, son, I do. I have loved your mother since the day I set eyes on her. I remember thinking, *Yes, sir, that is the woman I am going to marry.* When I told my parents, they told me it would never work." He loosened his tie and tossed it on the ground. "You see, your mother was and is a beautiful lady who knows what she wants, while I had my head in the clouds and wanted to make my own way. We were a lot like you and Beth actually. The point is that as a parent you may think you know what's best, but at some point you have to sit back and let them make their owns choices. I am sincerely sorry that I butted in your relationship. It will not happen again."

"It's over now, Dad. She hates me." I buried my face in my hands, and he patted me on the back.

"It's not over until you win her heart, son," He stood up slowly and walked to the elevator. I looked up and saw her standing a few feet in front of me. She must have never left the garage.

"Beth, please let me explain." I jumped to my feet and rushed to her.

"Camille already did."

"You spoke to her?" Shock, and fear for that matter, rippled through me like a tidal wave.

"Yes. She told me what you said about being in love."

Oh," I responded.

"She said that she had never seen you this torn up over a woman, even her." She put her hand on my cheek and gently caressed it. I let my head droop into her soft hand and tried to pray for the right words.

"I love you, Beth. I know this has been kind of a rocky start, but I am willing to work every day to show you that I am the man that you need me to be. Just let me show you."

She nodded her head. "Yes." I was so relieved that I had finally gotten through to her. I leaned down to kiss her, and she met me halfway. I lifted her up into my arms and carried her over to the benches in the garage. I held her there in my arms, and we talked about how we felt and what our next step was. I didn't care what came next as long as we were together. Beth had come back to me, and I was on cloud nine.

We spent that night at her place where we ordered Chinese food and watched movies. That night we made love—the passionate-mind-blowing-curl-your-toes kind. We lay in bed that night with her head on my shoulder and our bodies tangled up in each other.

"I love you, Drew." She was half-asleep when she mumbled the words. I was still reeling from the day's events drawing circles on her back with my fingers.

"I love you too." I kissed the top of her head and hugged her a little tighter.

Test Drive Complete- I found the one I want.

EPILOGUE

THE SUN BEAT DOWN on the dark fabric I was wearing. I stood at the end of a rose petal aisle where beautiful women were making their way to the altar. When Beth started down the aisle, I sucked in a deep breath. She looked beautiful wearing a daisy yellow dress with a bouquet of daisies at her waist. Her hair was perfectly in place with a pearl comb pushing back one side.

She faced me from across the altar and mouthed, "I love you."

I returned the sentiment as the ceremony got started. I had not even seen the bride walk down the aisle, but she and her beautiful flower girl, Emmaline, had made their way down, and she was now perched in front of the altar.

"We are gathered here today in the sight of God and these people to join together Matt Carlson and Victoria Dempsey in Holy Matrimony."

I got lost in the words and the tears streaming from Beth's eyes as she watched our two best friends get married. They had only met six months ago, but Matt said he knew this was the woman he was meant to be with.

Emmaline, Victoria, and Matt were a family now, and he had become quite the stepfather to little Emma. She adored him, and he was smitten by the talented little girl.

Jason nudged my arm, and I remembered the rings. The shiny ring caught the glare of the sun, and I almost dropped it onto the sandy beach.

Matt and Victoria were pronounced husband and wife. He kissed his bride and picked her up out of the sand. Georgia came up on cue with Acorn and Starlight in tow. As a special favor for the groomsmen, she had brought two of her finest horses for the wedding. I gave Starlight a pat on the back. Beth had given her a bath that day and her dark skin glistened in the setting sunlight.

Matt and Victoria climbed on top of the horses and headed off down the beach to the reception site at the hotel.

I thanked Georgia for the horses. "Anytime, Drew, except for Tuesdays and Thursdays. We received a donation from a company called Sloane Enterprises. Have you heard of them?" She winked. "They want to help us keep our equine therapy open. There is enough money that we could expand to adults with disabilities too. I don't know who they are, but they must care an awful lot about those kids."

"I have always said y'all have a special program out there. I am very happy for you." Georgia went to load up in her truck and go meet the bride and groom at the hotel. She had been all but gracious when I told her that I had already found the love of my life. She was a sweet girl, but Beth was the only girl for me. I sat down behind Beth on the sandy beach, and we watched the waves crash into the sand. The rest of the group walked down the beach, but the two of us were happy to be in each other's arms.

"Did I tell you that you're the prettiest woman here?" I said, covering her lips with my own.

"Yeah, I think you mentioned that once or twice."

About the Author

Avonlea Cole is a romance junkie from a small town. She started writing at an early age and has finally settled down to write out her own set of fantasy love stories. She is dedicated and driven with a love of happy endings. You can find her cuddled up to the computer or book or whatever she can find to read or write on. Avonlea is a wife, mother, author, and anything else she needs to be. Her books will leave you smiling as they inspire hope and happiness to its readers showing how perseverance and love can conquer all.

www.ingramcontent.com/pod-product-compliance
Lightning Source LLC
Chambersburg PA
CBHW070929130626
46555CB00001B/354